I0690747

The Fragile Things

The Fragile Things

MARY CANTELL

RESOURCE *Publications* · Eugene, Oregon

THE FRAGILE THINGS

Copyright © 2024 Mary Cantell. All rights reserved. Except for brief
quotations in critical publications or reviews, no part of this book may
be reproduced in any manner without prior written permission from the
publisher. Write: Permissions, Wipf and Stock Publishers, 199 W. 8th Ave.,
Suite 3, Eugene, OR 97401.

Resource Publications
An Imprint of Wipf and Stock Publishers
199 W. 8th Ave., Suite 3
Eugene, OR 97401

www.wipfandstock.com

PAPERBACK ISBN: 979-8-3852-1037-4
HARDCOVER ISBN: 979-8-3852-1038-1
EBOOK ISBN: 979-8-3852-1039-8

VERSION NUMBER 03/12/24

To my beloved husband, my love always,
and to the memory of my precious mother,
who nurtured the writing bud in me to bloom, thank you.

Above all, to my Lord,
who guides my mind and heart to write.

Acknowledgments

Andrew Fidler, Upper Merion Twp. Police Dept.

Dion Reid, Lifeline Medical Services

Blaine Leis, Upper Merion Twp. Police Dept.

Debra Culvar, PennStarr

Judi Mobley, editor

Trayce Duran, editor

Chapter One

June 6

6:43 p.m.

AN ODD FEELING CAME over Sarah the moment she walked into her apartment. She eased her feet out of her too tight shoes and dropped her purse and keys on the foyer table. Turning for her bedroom down the hall, her heart jolted at seeing something that defied all logic at the end of the hallway.

"Oh, my G—what in the world?" In shock, her gaze riveted onto scattered chunks of debris spread all over the polished hardwood floor. The porcelain from the cherished antique sculpture of her great-grandmother lay shattered at the foot of the open closet door like a cyclone had blown through the apartment. An icy chill tore through her as blood rushed to her face. "How did this happen?" The chaotic mess chafed her spirit—not only the effort it would take to clean it all up. . .no, it went beyond that. The beloved woman Sarah heard about in stories through the years was now reduced to mere rubble. Her life as a humanitarian, society matron, and her philanthropic identity were things Sarah admired. All that was left—the broken remains—lent zero respect for the once idolized woman. Sarah dropped to her knees as tears brimmed in her eyes.

"Hey, Mom," fifteen-year-old Emily called from the opposite end of the hallway. "Here's the receipt for the clothes you asked for. Mom! What happened?"

1

Emily's voice sounded distant as though it came through a long tunnel. Sarah could barely hear anything but the thoughts running in her head. *Did the statue fall by accident? Did someone throw it down on purpose—in anger, possibly?* She gently picked up one of the porcelain shards and hoped it could be pieced together again but soon realized the improbability. Some of the statue had crumbled into all but dust.

"Oh, Em, I just can't even fathom how this even happened?" She shook her head and stifled her desire to scream. As much as she wanted to keep the sculpture for sentimental reasons, she would have to deal with the loss. Though, thankfully, there were others items in her inheritance that may have been worth more than mere sentimental value, and she looked forward to getting the artifacts appraised—the silver, china, and oil paintings—to, hopefully, sell for some extra cash.

"Maybe, we could put it back together?"

Sarah slowly shook her head. "No, it'll be impossible."

"I'm so sorry, Mom."

"It's not your fault, Em." Sarah wiped her moist eyes with the back of her palm.

Sarah sighed and stared at the overwhelming sight, taking time to gather her thoughts. *Unbelievable. Who could have done this?* She surveyed the extent of the damage that covered the entire lower end of the hall and joined Emily in picking up the bigger pieces, setting them aside on top of the hallway table. She could toss them later. Right now, she didn't have the heart to do it.

After clearing most of the debris, she took out the vacuum cleaner and plugged it in. Exhausted from shopping all day, this wasn't the best time to tackle the chore, but her neat-freak sensibilities kicked in. It would be better to clean up the mess now than have to face the task in the morning.

"Thanks, Em. I can handle the rest. Why don't you just go put your new clothes away?"

"You sure, Mom?"

"I can finish up here. It's fine." As Emily went to her room, Sarah was about to flip the vacuum cleaner switch when something caught her eye. She stepped closer to the closet and peered inside. The back shelf, partially obscured in shadow where the rest of her inheritance had been stored, was empty. "What?" she cried. "Where's my other stuff?" Her favorite painting—the bowl of fruit—was missing, something she loved as a child. Viewing the painting when she visited her great-aunt's home in Florida gave her a rush. The life-like character of the subject matter drew her finger to the painting where the fuzzy peach appeared invitingly real. Sarah racked her brain thinking of where else she could have possibly stored the items rather than in the hall closet until reality hit: The sterling silver tea set, the silverware collection, and several Hummel figurines were gone. Stolen. She didn't know their exact worth, but they certainly were worth something. Of course, the Hummel collection was definitely valuable. Watching old artifacts being appraised on *Antiques Roadshow* enough times proved the worth of the pristine china figures. First, a priceless possession is destroyed beyond belief, and now the other treasures from her inheritance had disappeared. In the shadows of the dim hallway, curiosity crept over her. *What was next?*

Sarah's anger simmered just below the surface and took quick command. She marched down the hall to the front door and boldly jerked it open. She wanted to scream that she'd been robbed. Violated, in fact. Assault her treasured possessions and they might as well have assaulted her. Nothing unusual lingered in the hall-way. . .no lurking stranger or any evidence of a crime. Just an eerie kind of quiet.

Sarah's adrenaline surged and caused her body to tremble as she searched the entire apartment. . .poking into the closets, peering under the beds and every conceivable place to make sure she and Emily were safe and no one else was in the apartment—possibly hiding. With her mind in overdrive, she was relieved to find they were, indeed, alone. Though if the robber had been there, her courage would surely rise to meet her match, and she would do whatever it took to protect her family. Three years of karate lessons would, hopefully, give her a leg up in defending herself. Thinking she should call the police, her thoughts turned to her ex-boyfriend, Nick—a cop. This would be a good time to call for help—or a hug. But on second thought, no. She couldn't bear to see him now that they'd broken up. It would be too awkward. She immediately banished the thought and called the resident manager's office to report the incident. Sadly, for her, Nick Durham was history. No use worrying about the past now. There were bigger issues to solve than why their love went wrong.

****

"Did you call the police?" Her best friend Cindy Holden's voice pitched through the phone.

Still fueled with adrenaline, Sarah nervously threaded her hand through her hair. "No, not yet. I'm not sure if I should."

"Why?" Cindy barked. "I would. I'm sure that stuff was worth something!"

"I know, but I'm just a bit . . . oh, I can't even think straight right now. My nerves."

"I would call them, Sarah."

"I checked the entire apartment and then called the management office and left a message for Mr. Kramer. If he suggests that the police should enter the picture, I'll deal with it later." Sarah didn't want to let on the real reason why she didn't want the police involved and the possibility of Nick finding out. Reporting the incident to them would only cause her stomach to cinch even more amid its turbulence—especially, if they sent Nick over. He was the last person she wanted to deal with right now.

"Get a cup of echinacea tea in you or chamomile. It'll calm you down," her friend encouraged.

"I d-don't even know if I have any." As she walked to the cabinet, her legs still trembled. "I'm so rattled."

"Deep breaths, Sarah, take deep breaths."

"I know, I'm trying." Sarah inhaled—in-through-the-nose-out-through-the-mouth—as Cindy talked her down from the precarious ledge where she stood. Cindy's encouraging words sounded more like yammering through the phone; they barely registered to Sarah through the jangling of her distracted nerves. The rush of adrenaline kept her body shivering while her mind spun in a thousand directions. *Would the robber come back? Did he mean harm or was this a warning? Stay with me, Lord.*

"Hey, listen," Cindy continued. "If there's anything you need me to do, please let me know, okay?"

Silence.

"Sarah? Need me to come over?"

"Yes, yes, I will."

"You want me to come over?" Cindy repeated.

"No, no. I'll let you know—"

"By the way, the barbeque is tomorrow. Hope you, can make it. Food, fellowship, and fun. Should take your mind off this whole thing—at least for a few hours." Cindy paused. "Hey, you there?"

Sarah sighed. "Yeah, I'm here. Sorry. Listen, sounds great, but I gotta go."

"Okay, hang in there, Sarah. Things will look better in the morning. I'll be praying."

"Thanks, Cindy. I'll call you tomorrow."

When Sarah hung up the phone, she realized it would take more than a cup of tea to fall asleep tonight. True, the barbeque did sound nice, and she loved eating outside, but for now, it was too much to even think about tomorrow.

In her room readying for bed, Sarah reached into her bedside drawer for the sleeping pills. Through the miscellaneous junk that collected there, she rustled her hand around until she felt the bottle, only to find all that was left were a few tiny fragments of the little white pills. It had been a while since she needed to take a sleeping aid. Something triggered her insomnia that she'd never experienced before after the passing of her husband, Brian, five years ago. After slipping into her softest nightshirt, she headed for the kitchen to check once more for tea. Midway, she stopped at her daughter's door.

Sarah peeked through the doorway to Emily's room, not wanting to invade her daughter's personal space. "You doing okay, sweetie?"

Emily, lying in bed, glanced up from her phone. "Did you call the police?"

Sarah stepped into the room. "I've checked the apartment, so there's nothing to be afraid of now. I thought it best to report it to management first. I'll let them take over from there."

Her daughter's beautiful green eyes reminded Sarah of the startled countenance of a baby fawn when a beam of light hit. . .so vulnerable and unsure.

"Don't be afraid, Em." Sarah sensed her daughter's unease. She moved closer and crouched down at Emily's bedside. "Everything will be okay," she gently comforted, patting the bedsheet. "We're safe."

Emily's focus went back to the screen.

Sarah cast her gaze around the room for a moment. "Well, you need your sleep, honey." She eyed the girl's phone, hating new age technology. . .such a distraction for kids these days. "And don't forget hockey camp starts on Monday. You need to get your things ready soon. Should be fun, right?" Sarah kept her voice upbeat to help assuage any lingering fears that Emily may have concealed.

"I know," came her daughter's same distracted reply.

"And don't be on your phone all night, please."

Emily grunted something that sounded half-agreeable, so Sarah didn't balk.

"Love you, Em."

"Love you, too, Mom."

****

Sarah padded her way to the kitchen. She peered into all of the cabinets, one by one, hoping to find at least one tea bag somewhere. She spotted an old decorative tin but found nothing but a couple of creamers and sugar substitute packets. Adjacent to the tin, a box of chocolate fudge cookies beckoned. She thought better than to eat so late at night, but the cookies were calling her. She sat at the oak table and munched one after the other, letting the sweetness and crunch take over and lift the tension that held her nerves like a vice. In the silence, odd sounds inside the apartment startled her. First, the loud pop of the old refrigerator made her jump, and then a random breeze abruptly slapped the kitchen window shade and sent her nerves jangling. After consuming more cookies than necessary, Sarah put the box back in the cabinet and then checked the front door once more before going to bed. The chair placed under the doorknob would, hopefully, secure not only the apartment but her peace of mind.

On her way back to her bedroom, she passed by the closet in the hallway where her inheritance had been kept. A sense of unease swept through, and a bolt of shock seized her as she imagined a gnarled hand reaching out from the shadows. She mentally recoiled and steeled herself to reject the ghastly image. *Stop thinking about horror movies, Sarah. They're fiction.* Almost to the bedroom door, her foot landed on one of the errant shards the vacuum cleaner hadn't picked up. *Ouch, damn it!* She bent over and pried it out. *Will this day ever end?*

In bed, Sarah opened her Bible to the Twenty-third Psalm and read the text over and over, letting the words calm her spirit. Later, as the sedative effects of the sugar worked their way through her system, leaving her brain in a numbing fog, she reached for the cord to lower the window shade. Outside in the distance, a police car cruised down the main driveway around the building. Her mind turned to Nick. Once again, her thoughts were never far from him, like a revolving loop in her mind. She strained to make out the number marked on the side of the vehicle. Was it by chance his cruiser *#1872*? Even by the illumination from the halogen street lamp, she couldn't make out the number. *Was Nick patrolling the building or possibly checking up on her?*

Slipping back into bed, Nick's image floated in her mind. His dreamy light blue eyes captivated her, and his statuesque physique stirred her lust. Whenever he held her in his arms, she always wanted more of him. His caress just wasn't enough. Too bad the demands of his job: the long working hours, along with his occasional temper and some bad habits eventually wore away some of the patina of her longing. Lifestyle differences built up so much that they chipped away at their relationship until, one day, it went bust. "It's over," she said, begrudgingly. "I can't do this any longer." Nick's face remained stoic as she spoke, and the light went out of his eyes. She regretted the surge of emotion that had welled up inside her the night she yelled at him and caused him to leave—this time, for good. The indelible hurt in his eyes would forever sear her mind.

Sarah needed someone in her life right now, if anything, to protect her both physically and emotionally. Not only for herself but for Emily, too. Deep down, she'd wanted so much for Nick to be a father-figure to her daughter. They'd gotten along well enough, and she thought, finally, her family could be whole again. Without the support of a man, things could go south for a young girl like Emily, so headstrong and impulsive, she could easily go off course without the reins of a masculine influence.

As she lay under the sheet, her mind raced. Scenarios played out like a kaleidoscope of horror scenes from TV crime dramas where evil motives and human nature collided. She no longer watched those types of programs, especially late at night, because the stories haunted her long after she'd turned off the TV. Often, the culprits in the tragedies were those near and dear to the victim. Exes in relationships often played a part long after they separated. Sarah held her pillow tightly as thoughts of Nick surfaced again. If he had been involved in any way, the truth would come out sooner or later, but for now, she couldn't bear knowing. If he'd been the perpetrator, it would tear her apart. Better to leave it alone—for now—and let management handle it.

Nick would never do anything to harm Emily or her. *Would he?*

Chapter Two

June 7

5:49 p.m.

LATE AFTERNOON SUN SHONE like a blinding dart through the cloudless summer sky. The scent of charcoal permeated the air from the grill across from the patio where Sarah sat nursing a soft drink.

"Phew, that sun is strong," Sarah said, shielding her eyes with her hand.

Cindy fidgeted with the table's umbrella and adjusted the angle lower. "How's that for you?"

Sarah moved her hand away. "Much better, thanks."

"Ugh, I'm sweating." Cindy wiped her face with the back of her arm.

Sarah glanced at the temperature gauge on the side of the house. "No wonder we're sweating, it's still 89 degrees."

"Feels like Haiti," Cindy said, her brow wet from perspiration. "Joe, how's it coming over there?"

Cindy's husband donned a chef's hat and apron like he did every summer for the Holden family's annual barbeque. "Almost ready," Joe called through a puff of smoke. "I'll let you know."

"Okay. Need another ginger brew, Sarah?"

"No, I'm good, thanks." She held up the bottle. "Still have plenty."

Cindy smiled. "I'm so glad you came. . .had my doubts that you would."

Sarah nodded and took a sip. "Me, too." She wasn't too enthused to be in a social setting right now, preferring her own company, but breathing in the fresh air was way better than hanging out in her stuffy apartment.

"I'm so sorry for you, girl. I half expected you to stay home and lick your wounds."

"I wanted to. . ." Sarah fiddled with the label on the bottle. "But what would it change?"

Cindy gave a mock frown. "I know it sucks, but this, too, shall pass."

"Pffft." Sarah rolled her eyes. "I know, I know,"—she nodded—"that's my favorite saying. . .it's just hard to hear it coming back at me."

"Easy for me to say."

"It's just hard because I was really counting on the money from some of those antiques to pay off bills and all, plus I'd really like to move someday. The rent keeps going up, and I'm tired of pouring money down a rat hole."

"I know having a house has been your dream for so long. Maybe this is a sign to finally get out of there? I mean, if it's that easy to break into the apartment."

"I really *do* need to get out of there." Sarah lifted the bottle to her lips and swallowed the last of its contents. "And now there's more than one reason to do it. Would be nice if I could manage something before school starts. I'd hate to uproot Emily in the middle of a semester."

"There's a new condo going up over by the golf course. I saw it in the paper."

"You still get the paper?"

"Just the Sunday edition."

"I saw some construction going up. Didn't know it was a condo. But it's probably not in my price range."

"You don't know that."

"I forget the name of it. Do you remember?"

Cindy shook her head. "I'll go find the paper."

"Another minute and we'll be ready over here, Cin," Joe called from the grill. He gently poked a long-handled fork onto the hot coals. "Meantime, you might as well bring everything out now."

"Finally," Cindy said. "I'll be right back." She struggled out of the plastic chair and went inside the house. A minute or so later, she came back out carrying a large tray of burgers and hotdogs along with a relish tray and a wad of newspaper tucked under one arm.

"Your usual burger, Sarah?" Joe called, a plume of smoke engulfing him. "Medium rare?"

"Sounds good," she replied, thinking how sweet that he remembered. His soft spot for her had been there even as a kid. Sweet ol' Joey.

"Mom, come on in," called Emily from the pool.

Sarah quickly shook her head and called out, "Not now, but maybe later." The upbeat tunes of Adele filtered out from a big black boom box, punctuated by a chorus of cicadas making their own crescendo of sorts in the cover of the trees. Sarah worried the robbery impacted Emily on some emotional level or made her more skittish, but from the looks of her carefree head tosses and frequent giggling in the company of Taylor, the Holden's youngest daughter, Emily seemed to have put the incident behind her.

"Here ya go," Cindy announced on her way back to the patio. She plopped the newspaper's *House and Rental* ads on the table in front of Sarah before settling her rotund bottom down on the patio chair. "There's a couple of condos going up. Seems everywhere you turn, they're building something." She picked up an ice cube from the ice chest and ran it down her neck. "Food's coming up. Need another soda or anything else, hon?"

"No, no"—Sarah waved her hand—"I'm still good for now."

Cindy seemed to be trying her best to keep Sarah's spirits up as though food and drink would help assuage, if not change, the situation of last night. She'd always been that way, but there was really nothing anyone could do for her right now, though Sarah was grateful someone was trying.

"The water's awesome," Emily announced as she came up to the patio. "You should've come in, Mom."

Sarah pulled a pen out of her purse and circled something on the newspaper as Emily leaned over the table, dripping water.

"Honey, you're getting water all over the paper."

"Sorry." Emily stepped back and twisted her hair into a pony. "What are you reading?"

"Just some condo ads," Sarah replied, matter-of-factly.

"We're getting a condo?"

"Maybe—one day."

"You mean, we're moving?"

"You're moving?" Taylor asked.

"Are we, Mom?"

"It's something I've been considering." Sarah kept her eyes peeled to the newspaper.

"But I don't want to move." Emily folded her arms across her chest.

The apartment they lived in currently had been great when Sarah first moved in five years ago, but the steady rent increases over the years caused her to re-think her long-term financial picture. She inwardly sighed and didn't feel the need to explain to her daughter the decisions involving finances, much less equity. The lessons would be lost in translation to a teenager.

"I'm looking for a place where I can invest my money—for you—for your future," she said while continuing to peruse the paper. "You'll be fine, Em, whatever I decide to do, so don't worry. Your mom's got your back." Sarah reached out and held Emily's arm for a second to emphasize her sentiment. She sympathized inwardly with her daughter's yearning to remain rooted where she was. Relocating from the familiar was always a precarious bridge to cross, though Sarah held her tongue from lecturing on the principles of necessity and prudence and wasn't about to get into an argument today. With everything else on her mind, she didn't need to cause a rift with her daughter.

"Where's the condo?" Emily asked, winding her hair around her hand.

"I haven't decided yet exactly, but wherever it is, I'm not planning on moving too far away, so most likely you'll still be in the same school district, and you'll still get to see your friends," Sarah offered, hoping it was enough of a consolation to appease her daughter.

"You girls hungry?" Cindy asked.

"Starved," Taylor piped in. "When are we eating?"

"Food will be ready in a little while. Meantime, I'd love to be in that water. Wanna go in for a quick dip?"

Sarah waved off the invitation. "It's okay. I'm fine here."

"Aw, not even get your feet wet?"

"I'll be your lifeguard," Sarah said, trying to be funny as a polite way of expressing her disinterest. "Go on, don't let me stop you."

"Okay," Cindy replied and ambled across the lawn to the pool.

Sarah put the newspaper aside. Her mind drifted back to the long-ago summers when she'd worked as a lifeguard. Days on end, she watched kids frolic in the water and older, retired folks, who skittishly entered the pool one tiny step at a time. The most taxing element to the job required knowing whether the water needed more chlorine or a full backwash. If only her life could stay so serene as those drama-free days of pool sitting.

As the aquamarine water in the Holden's pool sparkled in the sunlight, the pleasant memories slowly faded and gave rise to her current situation. Intruding thoughts of her family heirloom lying shattered on the floor, along with the rest of the stolen items, pressed down like a wrecking ball. She made a mental note to check out the new condo at the first available chance, but without her antique inheritance to sell for cash, she felt her hopes dashed from the start. The most confounding thing was wondering who even knew she kept any valuables in the apartment? She hadn't told a soul.

"Ah, that felt good," Cindy said as she came back to the patio and shook her hair at the table. The sight of water spraying out from woman's close-cropped blonde perm reminded Sarah of her old yellow Labrador, Daisy, when it got wet in the rain. For the first time in a long while, she smiled.

The savory scent of grilled meat wafted in the humid air. Sarah got up and picked out another bottle—this one a hard brew—from the ice chest perched at the edge of the patio. She twisted off the cap and eyed the grill, longing for one of Joe's delicious burgers, hoping the food and drink would ease her anxiety level while allowing a respite from thinking about her problems.

"Ready!" Joe called, wiping his brow with the towel draped over his shoulder.

"Looks yummy," Sarah said, eyeing the sizzling burgers as she approached the grill.

"Pleasure's all mine, honey," he replied with a wink as he placed one on her plate.

Sarah then headed to the condiment table and layered the juicy meat with ketchup, mustard, and pickle slices. Back at her place under the umbrella, Sarah started eating, and thoughts of her ex-boyfriend floated through her mind again. He'd been on her arm at the last gathering Cindy and Joe hosted, and now with his absence, she felt odd without him, even though she initiated going their separate ways. Sarah felt guilty at the thought of telling Cindy her true feelings after it became a question of who could have stolen her things. How embarrassing would it be to tell Cindy that she'd been responsible for setting up her best friend with a possible thief?

Chapter Three

"So, THAT'S WHAT HAPPENED." Sarah made a face and shrugged.

"Aw, no!" Cindy's expression fell. "I thought you and Nick were doing so well. I'm so sorry, hon. I had such hopes for you guys. When did this happen?"

"A few of months ago."

"This is awful. I feel so terrible."

Sarah shrugged. "Well, you didn't do anything. This isn't *your* fault."

"I know, but I was hoping this would be a good thing for you—for both of you. Did he cheat or?"

"Oh, no"—Sarah shook her head—"nothing like that. It's just."

"I don't mean to pry, but—"

"No, no, it's okay." Talking about Nick just about broke her spirit altogether and brought back the memory of the day she told him goodbye. His eyes resembled a forlorn puppy. For a strong cop, his bravado masked his soft heart. "It was my idea"—she bore a mock frown—"Let's just say things just weren't working out. Nothing in particular, yet everything."

"I'm so sorry," Cindy mused. "I'm sure it hurts."

"Even worse to be the dumper." Sarah teased out a stiff smile to put a balm on the situation. Her heart hadn't mended as much as she thought, and now it felt like it was bleeding all over again. With his possible culpability in robbing some of her valuables by taking out his anger on being dumped, her feelings were tossed every which way like the spin cycle of a dryer.

"Come to think of it, he hasn't been in the café in a while," Cindy said. "He's probably drowning himself in his work, I guess. Poor guy. Hope he stays safe. . .such a dangerous job."

Sarah knew all too well the perils of being a cop. That was one of the sticking points in their relationship. Long hours, question-able safety. She needed a stay-at-home kind of guy whose moral support didn't have to be phoned in from a squad car at the corner of Dead End and Hold-up Street.

"Well, one thing's for sure," Cindy began, "he really cared about you. At least, that's what everyone said."

"I hope you're not trying to guilt me into going back with him?" Sarah said, lending a smirk.

"Just being real is all." Just then some of the other guests came through the gate. "Hey, guys, welcome! Glad you could make it," Cindy called out.

Sarah took a back seat to the chit-chat and merriment from the adjacent table. Cindy, always the life of the party, could manage holding everyone's attention with her quirky sense of humor. As the other neighborhood guests exchanged playful banter among themselves, Sarah listened from a distance to the small talk of their seemingly bliss-filled lives. Amid their laughter, she recoiled at hearing something that reminded her of Nick. Everything re-minded her of him now that he was gone from her life. His imprint came in songs on the radio, TV commercials, *Cops*, the police show. . . She couldn't get away from him.

As she finished her burger, the piercing screech of a siren cut through the neighborhood. It left her wondering if Nick had been on call today? Was he in hot pursuit of a thug or just a minor car accident? Or was he in the hospital due to a gun-shot wound? So much for pushing him out of her life.

Chapter Four

June 9

5:55 a.m.

SARAH TOSSED BACK AND forth in a restless sleep as her dreams morphed into nightmares. They carried her into the depths of a giant swimming pool where she fought to hold her breath while struggling to reach the surface. The fear of drowning terrified her. All night, the same restless battle with her subconscious raged and left her expended by morning. As sunlight slipped through the blinds, she bolted upright. The reality of a new day hit, and it took a while to let the demons of the night leave her brain.

Sarah glanced at the clock. At this hour, she didn't want to face the morning and would rather lie back down to snuggle into the softness of the bed covers. Maybe a second try at sleeping would lend to a more pleasant dream sequence and take her to a better place. But it was time to get up. Today, Emily was leaving for camp.

Padding her way down the hall to the kitchen, a sense of relief came at seeing the wooden chair she tucked under the door knob last night still in place. She was grateful there was only one entrance into her residence unlike her friend, Martina, who lived out in the country and whose home contained at least nine doors Sarah counted the last time she visited her friend in Chester County.

While the oatmeal simmered, she set the table, washed some berries, poured juice, and laid out Emily's vitamins. All the while she hoped her daughter was awake and there wouldn't be a struggle

17

to rouse her to get ready to board the bus for her week-long hockey camp.

Sarah stood at the threshold to Emily's room. She cringed at the disheveled chaos that was her daughter's style. Clothes strewn everywhere. . .dressing table cluttered. Looked like a flea market on a bad day. Sarah wondered how her daughter could ever find anything, and it brought to mind Sarah's old college roommate, who'd shared the same cluttered style. The two-person dorm room she once shared with Maddy Craven resembled the typical aftermath of a storm on the right side of the room vs. the clean-up on the left. Often, Sarah attempted to straighten things out for Emily, but inevitably, the clutter crept back into place like it had its own mind. Despite the clothes-strewn room, Sarah was pleasantly surprised Emily was up and dressed already. Her daughter's maturity in getting herself out of bed at the early hour without any intervention impressed Sarah. *Another milestone?* Normally, it would take no less than a crane to get her daughter to move before six a.m. The clutter was the least of Sarah's concerns; there would be plenty of time to straighten things up while Emily was away at camp.

Sarah stepped into the room and put her hands on her hips. "Got your things ready, Em?"

"I can't find my—oh, here it is." Emily grabbed her phone and zipped up her satchel.

"Don't forget your mouth guard and the shin protector things," Sarah said.

"I won't."

"Okay, well breakfast is just about on the table. Remember, the bus will be here by seven."

"Be there in a minute," Emily called out as Sarah went back to the kitchen.

****

The sultry summer humidity that morning hung like a thick quilt. Sarah waited with her neighbor, Beth, outside on the sidewalk of the apartment's circular driveway where the bus soon would pick up their girls for the hour-long drive to Bethlehem. Emily and Beth's daughter, Hayley, stood with two other girls from the neighborhood, who all gathered like baby chicks in a hen house. They chatted amiably in girl talk punctuated with awkward giggles as they compared their varied accessories in field hockey attire from colored sweat bands and shin guards to their polished hockey sticks; their innocence, still their best feature. Long-limbed and gawky, the hidden beauty they harbored would at any given moment turn from awkward adolescent to a blossoming flower. Each girl had potential, Sarah surmised—even Hayley. Actually, Hayley seemed to have a leg up on most of them. With her curvaceous body and long golden hair, she looked light years more grown-up than the average adolescent.

"It'll be a nice break for them," Sarah offered.

Beth lent a tight smile, and Sarah noticed the change in the woman's demeanor. Not like when Beth and Hayley first moved into the apartment next door. Beth used to have high spirits a few years ago. Now, she appeared weighed down by an invisible stone.

"It'll be good for them to hang out with their peers," Sarah added, glancing over to where the girls stood.

Beth chewed her lip. "I had to practically twist Hayley's arm."

"Well, they're at that age," Sarah reassured.

"I know but. . ."

"Well, at least, she's on board with it now, right?"

"At her counselor's suggestion—well, it was more like a mandate."

Sarah shot a glance to where the girls stood. All the more, Sarah resolved to support the woman whose wayward child underwent a lot of struggling this past year. Hayley was around Emily's age—about a year older, and they shared some commonalities that kept them friendly, including an equal disdain for science class. Sarah recalled the latest issue involving Beth's daughter and once listened as a teary-eyed Beth shared the story about the red nail polish that, apparently, Hayley used to feign suicide. Sarah shuddered as Beth told the story, and deep in her heart, she winced that a mother would be forced to go through the mental anguish of such a thing as sending her own daughter to juvenile hall.

"Oh, Beth." Sarah shook her head.

"Yep, poured it out the bottom of the door. All I could think of was that she'd sliced her wrists. . .can you imagine?"

Sarah's skin crawled at the image of *fire engine red* nail polish dripping off the white marble threshold of the bathroom. Poor Hayley. Poor Beth. Hopefully, the fellowship of school friends, coupled with fresh air and healthy activities during the week-long camp away from home, would be a blessing to Hayley and lend some order to her life. In the sporting arena of coaches and scrimmages, the girls would be kept busy with a full schedule. Learning the concepts of team work and competition would, hopefully, segue into applying the same concepts to broader challenges of life. Sarah would be adding Hayley to her prayers—if anything, to the top of the list.

In the distance, a yellow bus rounded the curve to the north driveway. Sarah glanced back at the girls. Her heart overflowed with pride. With pale translucent skin and auburn hair, her daughter appeared no less perfect to Sarah than an artist's figurine. Pure, innocent. The girl's budding curves in her petite figure mimicked Sarah's own at fifteen. How blessed she felt to have a healthy, happy daughter.

"Have a good time!" Sarah called. She wanted to shout, *I love you* and give her a hug but thought better not to embarrass her daughter. Better to let the apron strings loosen without knotting them up again. A bittersweet sensation tore through her. Cutting the apron strings somehow also cut into her heart as she watched the yellow bus pull out and disappear down the road.

Chapter Five

Nick Durham struggled to get out of bed. Stretched out in shorts and a T-shirt, he reached first for the pack of cigarettes lying on his bedside table. While about to light one, his thoughts turned to Sarah—again—and her words echoed in his head. *Those cigarettes are going to kill you one day.* She'd been on his mind since the day she ended thing between them. His relationship with Sarah Harding ended over two months ago, and it left him reeling ever since. Yet he couldn't bring himself to move on. In haste, he lit the cigarette. *To hell with her.* He inhaled deeply and soon began coughing. Bolting upright, he reached for the half-empty water bottle and gulped the contents down to stop the choking sensation. When the coughing stopped, he smashed the burning cigarette into the ashtray to snuff it out, and then grabbed the pack of remaining cigarettes and threw it across the room.

****

"Here's the case reports you needed," said Ginny Anderson, the precinct's administrative assistant. "Oh, and there's a *10–12* in the lobby. . .has a question for an officer. Apparently, no one else can help her.

Nick blindly stared at something on his desk.

"Nick?"

He looked up.

"There's a 10–12 in the lobby with a problem. By the way, what's *your* problem? You haven't been yourself in weeks."

Nick ran his hand through his hair. "Not a damn thing. . .nothing."

"Could've fooled me, Anyway, you gonna take it, or should I tell her no one is available right now?"

He blew out a breath. "I'll take it."

Ginny laid the papers in his in-box. "Got more where these came from. The Chief asked for you to review them before they get filed."

"Sure, fine," Nick mumbled to himself.

"You sure you're okay, honey?" she asked.

Nick didn't know what to tell her. Even if he knew where to begin, having to admit to being dumped wasn't something he wished to share—especially, to a woman. Truth be told, his heart felt heavy as granite these days. Breaking up with women became water under the bridge for him in the past with others. He'd hurt for a while, and then he bounced back. This break-up was different. No, his secret feelings toward Sarah Harding would remain private.

"Yep, I'm good," he said, rifling through his in-box. His mind wandered again. Who knew for how long he'd be able to be without her? Would his heart be permanently broken or just remain chafed until he met someone else? Only time would tell. Meantime, he poured himself into his menial work. It would distract him for a while but not for long. This woman forged a permanent mark in his heart and branded it with an invisible kiss. There would never be another Sarah Harding in his life no matter how long he searched. While his job as a cop was dangerous, his love life could be even more so. His heart was never more on the line than right now.

Chapter Six

SARAH STEPPED INTO THE Management office where the air conditioning blew at full blast. Cathy, the office secretary, sat typing at her computer.

"Morning, Cathy."

"G'morning." The elderly woman glanced up at Sarah.

Sarah let out an audible sigh and peered over the top of the gray-haired woman's head to the resident manager's office door. "Is Mr. Kramer in by any chance?"

Cathy paused from typing and looked up. "I'm pretty sure he hasn't left yet." She held up her index finger. "Let me check." She extended her arm toward one of the chairs lining the wall across from her desk. "Have a seat." On her way toward his office, she paused and turned. "Forgive me for being too pointed, dear,"—she pulled off her glasses—"are you okay? You look—well, you don't look your usual pretty self today."

Sarah blew out a breath. "Been better, thanks." As their eyes met, Sarah's reticence dissolved, like a pin had been stuck in her and the truth about the robbery slowly slipped through, waning under the pressure of the woman's sympathetic stare. "My apartment was ransacked," Sarah let out under her breath. Saying the words out loud was like a few heavy rocks in the load on her back fell away. Though she told practically every detail to her friend Cindy, sharing the info with Cathy felt as though the secret was really coming to light and no longer something that needed to be hidden.

"Oh, no! Good Lord. That's awful."

"Yeah, it was pretty shocking."

"Oh, yes, I'm sure it was."

"I left a voice message the night it happened—Friday."

"You did? Oh, I'm so sorry. I was just about to check the messages right after this emergency that came up. Anyway, I'm terribly sorry that I didn't get to it before you came in, Sarah. This is terrible to hear."

"Oh, no worries, Cathy. I'm dealing with it."

Cathy raised her index finger. "Hold on a second," she said and went to the back of the office.

As Sarah waited, her mind flew back to that awful night and her nerves tightened. The incident still had her rattled. Just thinking back on the odd feeling that came over her as she entered her unlocked apartment sent a shiver through her. Just then, Cathy came back around to her desk.

"Mr. Kramer can see you now, dear." Her eyes held a measure of sympathy.

"Thanks, Cathy," Sarah said and headed for the resident manager's office.

"I'm very sorry that this happened, Sarah. It's quite disheartening, I'm sure." Mr. Kramer eyed her with fatherly concern from behind his desk. "I must say it's the first robbery we've had, at least since I've been manager here." His expression bore a sober commiseration, reminding her of a forlorn dog as the creases between his eyes deepened. "We'll get your lock changed as soon as possible." He slapped his hands together over the desk top. "In fact, I'm going to handle it right now." He picked up the phone receiver. "Should be done later this afternoon. If all goes well, you can pick up your new keys from Cathy by 5 o'clock."

"Thanks, Mr. Kramer." Sarah forced a weak smile as she stood to leave.

"You bet'cha," he said with a decided nod.

Sarah's heart lifted as she left the management office. She felt lighter knowing that Mr. Kramer would take swift action to remedy the situation.

Chapter Seven

SARAH STOOD IN THE lobby waiting for the mailman to finish stuffing the rows of boxes in the mail room. From where she stood, it didn't look like much of anything important was inside the long narrow compartment. Aside from junk mail circulars and flyers, the only thing she found worth keeping was a New Homes real estate brochure and a bill. As she turned to leave, her neighbor, Winny Sterns, hobbled across the marble-floored lobby toward the mailroom.

"Oh, there you are. Sarah. Are y-you alright? I heard about someone trying to break into your apartment!" The pace from Winny's palsied speech was somewhat slow, but her mind remained as sharp as they come. "Is this true?"

"Oh,"—Sarah made a face—"thanks, Winny," she replied with a nod. *News travels fast around here.*

"I'm so sorry to hear about this."

"Yes, but we're okay." Sarah wasn't going to let on about the actual details of the robbery. For all anyone knew, it was just an attempted break-in or a minor one—at worst case, one with nothing much stolen. That was the story Sarah stuck with so as to not burden any of the residents unnecessarily, especially Winny. The poor woman bore enough concerns as it was than to bear Sarah's, too, in light of John Sterns, Winny's caretaker, who acted more like a disciplinarian than a brother.

"Must've been awful."

Sarah nodded. "A bit much, yeah, but we'll be okay."

"How is Emily?"

"Em is fine. She's at hockey camp for the week," Sarah explained. "Up in Bethlehem."

"That's good"—she nodded—"I'm glad. This world. . .I dunno."

"And how are you?" Sarah asked, changing the subject.

"Getting by, I guess." She pointed to her cane. "Wish I didn't need this, but what's an old woman gonna do, right?" She mocked a laugh.

"Oh, Winny, you're definitely not old!"

"Compared to you," she said. "So, you're moving?" the woman asked with a frown, as she pointed to the New Homes brochure in Sarah's hand.

"Well, I'm not sure. Right now, it's just an idea. I may not be able to afford to move right now."

Winny's eyes softened. "I hope you don't move, Sarah. You're one of the bright spots in this whole building."

Sarah smiled. "Aw, you're so sweet, Winny, but we'll see. I'm still sorting out my fund situation. I'm having some financial concerns. So, no, it's not a done deal yet, Win. But I won't forget you if I do move. I'll keep in touch. You can be sure of that." Sarah gave Winny's shoulder a gentle squeeze to drive home the point.

"So, you'll give me your address when you move?"

"Of course, why wouldn't I?" Sarah witnessed the tears in the woman's eyes. "Now, please don't cry, Winny. You're going to make me cry." Sarah offered a feigned chuckle to help lighten the situation. "Besides, I haven't moved *yet*."

"Oh, I don't like change. . ."

"Aw, listen. . .I know"—Sarah put her arm around the woman's shoulder—"nobody does, but you'll be okay."

Sarah walked with Winny to the mailroom and chatted with her while the woman retrieved the contents of her mail box. Then she escorted her to the waiting elevator and entered. When the elevator arrived at the fourth floor and they stepped out to walk down the hall, Winny's brother, John, stood outside his apartment door with his arms crossed over his chest like a disgruntled sentry. He bore an icy stare.

"Hey, John," Sarah said, keeping her tone upbeat and hoping to counter the man's defensive posture. "So sorry to have kept your dear sister so long. We've been chatting downstairs," Sarah offered, hoping to appease his stone-like demeanor. His features looked carved by a chisel.

"Yeah, I figured." His voice, dismissive. He cast his gaze on his sister hobbling up behind Sarah as they came down the hallway. "C'mon, Winny. Doctor's appointment at 1 o'clock," he called with a beckoning wave."

Winny nudged her cane forward and began to head to the door. "Oh, yes, I almost forgot."

"I'm sorry, John, if I held her up," Sarah repeated. She reached out to support her friend's awkward gait as she double-timed her steps.

He stood stoic with his hands now placed on his hips. As the poor woman made her way along, John held a steely stare that reeked of disdain. Sarah couldn't figure out whether his attitude was directed toward her or his sister. Either way, his vibe cut through her like a knife.

Chapter Eight

"HEY, UNCLE HARRY, THAT was too generous of you!" Sarah gushed over the phone. "I just noticed the filet mignon in the freezer yesterday. You're so sweet to give it to us."

"Glad to do it, honey, and sorry I missed y'all."

"Oh, we would have loved to have seen you."

"Well, me, too. That's why I came over." He chuckled.

"I'm so sorry our timing isn't better." She glanced at the clock, hoping this wouldn't be one of her uncle's long phone calls. God love him, the man could talk. "So, when did you stop by?"

"Well, uh. . .let's see. . .I believe, Friday. Yep. Stopped by right after closing the shop. When you didn't answer the door, I just let myself in and put the meat in your freezer."

A chill ran through her. *The day of the robbery?* It was only then that she realized she'd once given Uncle Harry a key. So, another person possessed the key to her apartment in addition to Nick and the management office. Sarah now added her own godfather to the list of potential intruders and possibly the one to have taken the missing items of her inheritance. *Fist Nick, and now Uncle Harry?* No way. The thought was ludicrous. She hated herself for thinking that way.

"It was weird though. When I got up to your floor, there was some kind of commotion in the hall."

"Oh?"

29

"Yeah, some yelling. . . someone cryin' something awful. . . a German Shepherd. . .the whole works. Like something out of a movie."

Sarah's mind raced trying to put the puzzle together. What really happened and who had been involved? It could have been just about anyone, although her neighbor, Beth, came to mind because they own a German Shepherd. Beth's daughter, Hayley, was no stranger to drug issues, Beth quietly let on to Sarah one day last year. Beth had a lot on her plate and bore the burden of raising Hayley alone most of the time while Tim, her husband, was away on business. Sarah thanked God that her own daughter, thus far, had been immune to those sorts of problems. Maybe there had been some sort of trouble with Hayley?

"And just when I was leaving, the dog came barreling down the hall," Harry continued. "Darn near ran me over. Got so un-nerved by it, I don't remember if I even locked the door behind me. And I accidentally dropped the key you gave me, I think, be-cause now I can't find it. Looked everywhere. I'm so sorry, honey. I searched all around for it. I think it bounced on the threshold and must have slipped back under your door is all I could figure."

Struck again by the memory of the break-in, Sarah's stom-ach tightened. Certainly, Uncle Harry wouldn't be on the radar as far as stealing from her. He wouldn't even take a free lunch and bore the responsibilities of a father figure to her after her beloved husband died, keeping her company. . .taking her and Emily for afternoon drives to the country. . .having them over to his house where he prepared his special southern style spare ribs the way only he could do. No, Uncle Harry wouldn't hurt a fly. They didn't come any more generous than Harry Fields.

Sarah pictured the key clanging on the black granite slab at the door's threshold and taking an awkward bounce. *So, where was the key now?*

"I'm so sorry about that, sweetie." His voice waned in regret.

"It's okay, Uncle Harry. Not a problem," she said, hoping to assuage the man's guilt in losing her key. Inwardly, the situation left her puzzled as she hadn't seen a key anywhere near the door.

Though arriving home that evening, exhausted from the day's shopping and errands, a loose key lying on the floor at the entry way would still be noticed; it would attract anyone's attention. So, that explains why the door was unlocked. *But where was the key?*

Chapter Nine

EMILY SAT CROSS-LEGGED ON the bench watching the field hockey scrimmage. In the 90-degree heat, beads of perspiration ran down her face and neck as though she just showered. After alternating the half-back position with Taylor Holden, the coach pulled Emily off the field for a break. During the time-out, she gulped as much water as she could, and even then, it barely quenched her thirst. Her clothes practically melted into her skin. She readjusted her headband that was wet enough practically to wring out and longed to get back into the game—or dive into the nearby pool. She glanced over at her friend, Hayley, who sat next to her on the bench. Hayley's face shone red as a beet after coming off the field from her goalie position.

"Ugh," Hayley uttered.

"What?" Emily replied.

"*This.*"

"The heat? Yeah, I'm sure it's awful playing with that mask on."

Hayley pointed to the field and frowned. "This whole thing."

"It's just hockey camp not manual labor." Emily wondered where Hayley was coming from and reached for a bottled water from under the bench. "Want a water?"

Hayley nodded and held her hand out.

"You make it sound like jail."

"It is."

"So, why'd you sign up for it?"

Hayley shrugged. "My mom—"

"Keep your eye on the ball, girls," shouted Coach Kearns. "Hustle, ladies, c'mon." She blew the whistle. "Off-sides, number four. Remember not to get distracted out there. Be where your feet are—always."

"A whole week of this?" Hayley said and took a swig from the bottle.

"The heat or the camp?"

"Both," Hayley replied, pouring the remaining water in the bottle down the back of her neck.

"Corner!" the coach called.

Beyond the field, the parking lot sizzled like a griddle as waves bounced off the surface. The unrelenting sun streamed down, baking the cars as though they were in a frying pan. The whistle blew and Coach Kearns beckoned everyone in.

"Good job out there, ladies. Let's call it a morning."

"Thank God," Hayley said.

"When do we get to use the pool?" the girl who played first string fullback asked.

Coach Kearns glanced at her watch. "Actually, right now, if you want to, and lunch is at noon. Everyone, please meet at Collier Hall. The cafeteria is on the first floor." She flashed a neon-white smile and patted her face with the towel around her neck. "Also, you can swim during your free time at four o'clock, right before dinner." She picked up her clip board. "You all did a great job for your first skills session. See you all after lunch for session two."

Hayley wiped her face with her sleeve. "Can't wait to peel these clothes off and go have some real fun."

"What are you talking about?"

"Fun. You know." She smiled.

"What kind of fun?"

"I'll tell you later."

Chapter Ten

SARAH'S MIND WHIRLED IN an endless loop of thoughts all night, lending little in the way of restful sleep. As the morning sun broke through the blinds, she awoke in a listless fog, not wanting to move. Eventually, she forced herself out of bed and boiled water for coffee. While waiting, she picked up the phone and placed a call to her boss at the hospital to request a couple of days off to mentally unwind and get some order back to her life. Right now, her mental footing felt about as secure as standing on the starboard side of a ship in a storm.

Sarah got dressed and afterwards decided that some good old mindless, menial labor might help get some perspective. She tackled Emily's room first, and took to straightening up the aftermath of what resembled a hurricane. Then she retrieved a dust rag from the laundry closet and dusted the living room while doing a load of laundry. During the drying cycle, she picked up the real estate brochure lying on the end table and paused to peruse it again. The condo ads inspired her; with names like Fox Meadow Estates, Arbor Crest Woods, and Blue Hill Reserve, each one captivated her senses and summoned a peaceful, if not quaint Americana feeling, so far removed from her present circumstances. Noting the listings were located not too far away from her present apartment, Sarah's heart lightened with the hope her next residence could be one of them. She embraced the idea until reality set in: *Do I have enough money?* Despite the bitter truth that she'd probably never get her inheritance back, she was determined nevertheless to go ahead and follow her heart.

****

Sarah's pulse rose as she stepped into the lobby of Greenleaf Realty. The well-designed office evoked the warmth of a home fresh out of the pages of *Architectural Digest*. Bright open window space lent sunlight for the sun-loving plants dotting the tables as it poured over the slate floor. While waiting to speak with someone, something drew her back. A bit apprehensive as though navigating into uncharted waters, second thoughts about purchasing a condo hit. In the wake of uncertainty, her initial enthusiasm waned. *What am I doing?* She never purchased real estate before. The only home she knew was Brian's, who bought his shaker roof Cape Cod long before they wed. It was perfect for them and even afterward with the birth of Emily. Though when he passed away, there was no way she was able to continue living with the shadow of his spirit behind every door. The funds she received from selling the property after paying off the mortgage were less than what she'd hoped for and now served as a small reserve for emergencies. The reserve grew smaller as time passed. *Will I be able to afford this?*

"Someone helping you?" a perky voice spoke in her direction.

Sarah looked over to see a woman now standing behind a sleek, elongated desk.

"Yes, I'm scheduled for an appointment with Evelyn Klein."

"Oh, okay." She looked down at the console phone. "I see she's on a call right now. Just a minute and I'll let her know you're here. . . Ms.?"

"Sarah Harding."

The woman lent a professional smile and slipped around the corner.

Sarah exhaled a breath and began pacing the lobby. After a minute, the click of high heels came from around the corner as a tall woman emerged.

"Hello," the woman said, lending a cordial smile, and with a slight cock to her head, she extended her hand. "I'm Evelyn Klein."

"Hi," Sarah replied and joined her hand to the woman's.

"So, you're interested in a condo. . .in this immediate area as I recall?"

"Yes, I had my eye on the one up by the golf course."

"Ah, yes. Greenbrier Hills. Come on back." She beckoned with a wave of her perfectly polished pink acrylic nails. "Let's talk in my office."

****

Sarah left the real estate office beaming with delight. On the way home, she called Cindy.

"So, yeah, I decided to go to a real estate agent this morning and guess what? The woman said she can put me into an FHA loan, provided I'm pre-approved," Sarah gushed.

"You went to a Realtor?"

"Yep."

"Good for you, woman," Cindy said, brightly.

"The only down side she mentioned was that it's not a buyer's market right now."

"Well, there's a good chance you could still get it," Cindy encouraged. "Maybe even with a seller's assist. Our neighbors next door. . .you met them at the barbeque. They got help."

"Assist. . .as in money assistance?"

"Yeah, the realtor didn't mention it to you?"

"They can do that?"

"The Jamisons got one."

Sarah's hope renewed at the same time the agent's words echoed in her head. . .*in this market. . .well, it's not the best. You'll need to make a decision fast or be left out. . .*

"So, listen. Do you want to go take a look at the condo with me?"

"Sure. . .when?"

"Soon as possible. How's tomorrow, bright and early?"

"You're not working?" Cindy inquired.

"No, I took a few days off. . .needed to get my head together. So, what time can I pick you up?"

"Let's meet in the morning. I've got the late shift tomorrow."

"Okay, sounds good. I'll pick you up. . .say between 9 and 10 a.m.?"

"Make it nine-thirty?"

"Works for me."

"Great, see you then."

Chapter Eleven

THE DORMITORY HOUSED ALL twenty-eight of the girls registered for the NCFH camp on the ground floor of the girls' wing of Mc-Millan Hall on the Moravian University campus in Bethlehem as they had done for the past decade. Emily and Hayley shared a room while Taylor roomed across the hall with a girl from another school. The dorm buzzed with the spark of teenage energy. Emily and Hayley laid on their fold-out beds on opposite sides of the room while Hayley took a drag from her cigarette.

"Ah, one day down, four to go," Hayley said through a cloud of smoke.

"Are we allowed to bring cigarettes in here?" Emily waved her hand in front of her nose.

Hayley blew out a smokey breath. "Don't know, don't care."

Hating the smell of cigarette smoke, Emily got up and opened the window. The air was so thick with humidity, nothing moved in or out of the room, and the smell stagnated. Attempting to breathe shallowly, she turned on the fan that sat under the window sill.

"Dinner's in an hour. Think I'll take a shower first," Emily announced as she gathered her toiletries, soap, and towel.

"Yeah, I need one, too," Hayley replied through the smokey air. "But I really don't want to eat dinner in the cafeteria."

"Why not?"

She snuffed out the cigarette and shrugged. "Just don't."

"I'm sure the food isn't that bad."

Hayley sprung up from the bed. "Listen,"—her eyes widened as she spoke—"we've got the whole night to ourselves. Why don't we head into town?"

"What's in town?"

"The Stacks."

"What's that?"

"You've never heard of the Stacks? It's cool. There's music—you know, bands and stuff."

"I don't know, Hayley"—Emily scrunched her face in disdain—"how would we get there?"

"I heard it wasn't far. . .we can walk."

Emily moved toward the door.

"Aw, come on. It'll be fun. You can eat in a crummy ol' cafeteria any day."

Soap, towel, and flip flops in hand, Emily opened the door.

"What d'ya say, Em?" Hayley's eyes danced.

Still reticent, she turned back and said, "I'll think about it."

****

The scent of barbequed beef filtered through the sultry air, and the thrum of music from the Hard Rock Café blared. Towering in the distance, two faded gray smoke stacks stood tall and proud as though propping up the cloudless sky. Like sentries from a long-ago duty, they'd been a fixture in the old steel town of Bethlehem, Pennsylvania, serving now as a remnant to call back the bygone prominence of a once glorified steel industry.

A strip of trendy stores and eateries lined the main street already filled with revelers. To the left, a group of twentysomething guys leaned against a wall sipping from plastic cups as they eyed half-dressed females passing by. A cacophony of steely electric music bounced off the hot cement farther down the block. A brightly lit Ferris wheel turned in the distance high above the open market. The district had blossomed from an industrial ghost town to a carnival of entertainment. Above it all, the lingering early evening sun kept the humid air hot and thick as batter.

All at once, Emily felt she'd taken a step into another world from her sheltered one. Feeling grown-up and free, it all swept her up into a new kind of high she'd never experienced before. In the rush of the crowd and the bright lights, the raucous atmosphere lent an air of the unknown. As though tittering on the edge of an enormous canyon, she couldn't help but step toward the edge and wonder if she could fly?

"Let's get a beer," Hayley announced, beckoning with her hand.

A butterfly sensation danced in Emily's stomach. *Beer?* She'd never had anything alcoholic other than a one-time sip from Uncle Harry's beer mug when she was seven or eight at a family Christmas gathering. Curious about the taste of the foamy, golden liquid, she asked him if she could have some. Finding the taste of alcohol not to her liking, her curiosity about it drowned in her first, bitter swallow. *Is this what adults like?* Rather than be a downer for Hayley or look like a child, Emily hesitantly followed the girl's lead to the Hard Rock Café.

Chapter Twelve

"Hey, there," came a male voice behind them after they stepped into the café. Two guys—one blonde and one dark-haired—stood eyeing them. Emily watched Hayley's expression turn from curiosity to a slightly sly smile. *Did she know them?*

"Hey," Hayley replied with enthusiasm, lifting her eyebrows as in surprise.

"I'm Jake. This is Trevor," the blonde said. He glanced from Hayley to Emily and then back to Hayley, where his eyes remained fixed.

Emily didn't like the vibe. Not at this point. She clutched her throat with her thumb and index finger, running them up and down, unconsciously. *What had Hayley gotten them into?* These boys were older, probably college age, and while Emily felt herself wading into deep water, Hayley seemed to be floating in a familiar pond.

"Buy you something to drink?" Jake asked Hayley with a quick glance at Emily.

"Sounds great," Hayley replied with a grin. "I'll take a beer." She turned to Emily. "You with me, Em?" she asked, giving Emily a light punch in the arm.

Blood rushed to Emily's face. Yet she managed to utter words that tripped over her tongue. "Sure, I-I guess I'll take a beer."

The two boys sidled up to the bar while Emily and Hayley stood behind them.

"Is this cool or what?" Hayley said with a giggle.

Emily wondered how things managed to stack up so perfectly for them to get drinks so easily. *Did Hayley plan this chance meeting?* Emily could only imagine as she held her arms protectively across her chest.

"I don't know, Hayley. These guys are—"

"They're great. Free drinks, Em! How can you beat that?"

"But I don't drink, Hayley."

Hayley smirked. "Well, up 'til now, maybe." She swiped her bangs out of her eyes. "Don't be a wuss, Em. Give it a try."

Her mind shot back to the first time where she felt uncomfortable around the opposite sex—the time an older boy approached her at a roller skating rink.

"Do you want to dance?" he rolled up to ask. The odor of cigarette smoke wafted in with him. As much as she loved to skate, having a boy by her side on the floor took her by surprise. His invitation sent her nerves jangling, and she shook her head—too shy to accept—and scooted away as quickly as possible.

"Here you go, ladies," Jake said, holding two mugs. He handed one to each of them.

Emily's nerves danced as she took hold of the frothy amber glass. Hayley's comments moments before swam in her head. Not wanting to embarrass herself, she took a small sip.

"But where's yours?" Hayley asked.

"Right here," Trevor announced as he handed a beer mug to Jake and quickly took a chug of his own. "There's a table right over there. Let's grab it."

Hayley took a sip and followed Jake and Trevor while Emily trailed behind. She struggled to keep up with them in the sea of bodies jostling each other as though in a tide pool.

"Oh, sorry," a tall girl shouted back to Emily after bumping into her, sending beer sloshing out and down the side of her glass.

Emily didn't care that the glass was now somewhat less full. She hadn't planned on drinking it anyway. The first sip tasted bitter to her, so there was nothing lost. It tasted much the same to her as it did when she was a little girl sampling her uncle's mug. . .like battery acid fluid.

In the shadows of the dimly lit room, the four sat around a small table. Loud music pulsed all the way through Emily's bones. She watched Hayley giggle and sip while basking in Jake's attention. Emily tried to reply to Trevor's remarks when he spoke into her ear, but shouting back through the screeching music seemed fruitless. By the time Hayley's glass was nearly empty, Emily hoped her friend wouldn't ask for or be offered another. Hayley may have been older, but she was still not old enough. Emily tried to catch Hayley's eye to signal that she wanted to leave. She needed food—not alcohol—and was dying for a burger.

"Wow, this beer is going right through me," Hayley said as she tried to scoot out from behind the table.

"Yeah, me, too," Emily chimed in as an excuse to get up from the table and leave the boys behind.

"Hurry back, ladies," Jake called through the din.

The girls followed the sign for the ladies' room where a short line of women queued up by the door. "Hope this line moves fast. . .I'm dying," Hayley said, fanning her face.

"Listen, Hayley—"

"So, you having a good time?" Hayley asked, pushing the hair off of her face."

"Actually, no. I want to go back to the dorm. Well, I want something to eat first. . .then go back."

"So, order something, girl."

"There's nothing here for me—just a bunch of fried stuff, fish, and—well, I've been hankering for a burger. There's a White Dog Grill I noticed on the plaza."

"But Em, we're having fun here. You're such a downer."

"*You* might be, but this. . .this just isn't for me, sorry."

"But why not? You got something better to do at that stale old dorm?"

"I just want to go is all. Does there have to be a reason?"

"Haven't you ever been on a date before?"

Emily declined to answer. Though she did kiss a boy when she was eight-years-old while playing house one summer. So, she wasn't exactly a prude. That mutual exchange could have been considered a date, but Emily knew the innocence of a kiss at eight wasn't really the same. There were no expectations nor a future with Barry Burk, just a kid's version of playing house on a lazy summer day. At the rate her friend was going, who knows what would happen if she actually got drunk? Unless she already was?

"So, what do you think of the guys?" Hayley asked on their way back to the table. "I really like Jake."

"They're okay. But. . .like I was saying—"

"Wanna hang with them? I mean, go out. . .you know, around town?"

"Hayley, like I told you, I'm hungry. . .and sweaty, too." She pulled her T-shirt away from her body and waved it. "I'm sorry to be a downer, but. . ."

Hayley stood with her hands on her hips. "Aw, Em, just a little while longer."

"Hey, if you want to stay, it's okay. I'll just walk back alone. It's fine. I don't mind."

Actually, it wasn't fine. Emily didn't really know which way to take back to the college campus. Hayley had led the way, and they were talking so much that Emily didn't pay much attention. Before going back to the table, Emily stood firm on her decision to leave. She hoped Hayley wouldn't call her bluff and let her go back alone. It wasn't a far walk, only about 20-minutes or so. If only she knew the way.

Hayley made a face and then palmed Emily's shoulders. "Okay, okay, we'll leave. But you owe me big time, Em. Just re-member this favor."

"Got it," Emily replied, relieved at being able to go. The two guys they'd met didn't impress her in the least, and between the loud music, warm beer, and the heat, this was all like a bad dream.

"Hey, guys," Hayley announced as she and Emily returned to the table where Jake and Trevor sat.

"Hey, sweetie," Jake said, raising a fresh mug of beer to his lips.

"Listen, we've gotta run, now." Hayley lent a mock frown.

"What for?" Jake replied. "You chicks meeting up with someone else?"

Hayley giggled. "No, no." She flashed a smile. "My friend. . ." She gestured with her thumb.

Emily grabbed the sleeve of Hayley's T-shirt and gently tugged to get her attention. "Come on, Hayley."

"Sorry, we gotta run," Hayley called with a wave.

"You serious?" Jake said. His expression turned sour. He banged down his mug. "We were just getting to know ya."

Hayley shrugged her shoulders. "We'll be back"—she glanced at Emily—"like tomorrow night, maybe. Right Em?"

Emily turned even more uncomfortable now and wanted to disappear. She'd never been referred to as a *chick* before and didn't know how to process it. She was sure Hayley could handle it; obviously, a year older, she'd been around the block, or so it seemed to Emily and probably more experienced. To Emily, Jake's eyes held a menacing glow in the dim lights, like a wolfhound or tiger. *Was he drunk?* She couldn't tell, but if anyone were a *chick*, it certainly wasn't her. Unless, of course, teeth with braces was the look he was after. Another reason to get out of there.

Chapter Thirteen

THE NIGHT PULSED WITH energy. Emily felt a heady rush to be out on her own, especially at this hour. The pungent aroma of sizzling beef permeated the air. . .piercing high-pitched screams came from the circling Ferris wheel. . .neon lights cast a carnival of colors everywhere, and the sweet scent of perfume drifted in the warm shadows of the evening.

"There's the White Dog," Emily said, pointing across the plaza. The girls stopped and ordered hamburgers and sodas. They brought their food outside and took a seat on one of the benches.

"Yum," Emily said. "I love eating outside."

"Yeah, it's pretty good. I could use a smoke though." Hayley looked around the plaza.

"How long have you been smoking?" Emily asked through a mouthful.

Hayley shrugged. "A while. . .at least a year."

"What does you mom say about it?"

"She doesn't know."

Emily was shocked that she could keep it a secret.

After finishing their meal, the girls walked around the plaza. Haley gestured toward the Smoke Shop. "I need to get more cigarettes. I'm running low."

"Hayley, you're underage," Emily scolded. "Besides, it feels late. Shouldn't we be getting back now?"

"What time is it?"

Emily brought out her cell. "It's almost nine."

"That all?" Hayley tossed her soda cup into a trash receptacle. "It's not late."

"We have practice in the morning, don't forget."

"Ugh, that *camp*."

"It's really not that bad. I don't know why you hate it so much." Hayley rolled her eyes.

"Well, my feet are getting sore," Emily said, hoping this would encourage Hayley to take them back to the camp. "I wanna go now. C'mon, let's go."

"Okay, fine."

****

"I hope we remember how to get back," Emily said after they'd left the entertainment district and had been walking for a while. "Are you sure this is the way?" She didn't pay much attention to the route Hayley led them on their way up to the Stacks. She'd been more concerned about whether they'd be caught skipping out of dinner with the others at the camp.

"Yeah, I'm pretty sure." Hayley drew out her last cigarette and lit it. She exhaled and turned her gaze from one side of the street to the other. "It's gotta be this way." She pointed to the left. Emily wasn't sure but took Hayley's word for it.

Row upon row of houses—some converted commercially into stores—lined the darkening streets in the neighborhood. The clusters of people grew less and less dense the farther they walked, and soon Hayley and Emily were just two of only a few others on the street. The night air remained thick, and the bass beat from one of the rock bands thumped in the distance.

After a while, a sense of dread welled up inside Emily. "Feels like we've been walking around in circles. Are you sure we're going in the right direction?"

"I thought it was this way," Haley replied, pointing down the street.

They stopped mid-way along 3rd street where most of the commercial district's storefronts, including a tanning salon, a hardware store, and a boutique shop were all closed and dark inside. The only place open for business was Pasquale's Pizza. The orange-red neon outline of a pizza glowed in the front window. As they passed, Emily noticed there were no customers inside and the frame of a short man could be seen behind the counter.

Farther down, a stone church draped in ivy appeared gothic in the dim shadows. Emily's gut told her something was wrong. "I don't know. . .I think we're going in the wrong direction. I think we're heading toward the river."

"I'm no good at directions," Hayley said, stomping out the cigarette. "Sorry."

Emily took the unofficial lead down the street and turned at the corner of 3rd and New Streets. Not knowing if this was the correct way back to campus, she took a gamble and headed east onto New Street where the breeze carried the subtle scent of lichen and green vegetation. The girls traversed another quarter-mile or so until Emily slowed her pace. "This still doesn't feel right, Hayley."

"Just keep going," Hayley replied. "We can't be that far off."

In the near distance, life-sized statues of people dotted the open space of brick pavers.

"They look so real, don't they?" Hayley said. "It's like they're staring back."

Emily ignored her. Ogling statues wasn't her idea of fun, especially while lost at night. Set on getting back to the campus was her main priority. Being out alone in a strange city was scary enough without any additional threats.

"They might just be staring at us," joked Hayley as they walked past the darkening figures. "Their eyes look like they're following us." Hayley reached out and grabbed Emily playfully by the neck. "Oooo," she uttered.

"Stop it!"

"Scared?" Hayley chuckled. "Em, you're such a nerd. Just chill out."

Emily swallowed her fear and trudged on. After a while, the heel of her foot began to chafe as it rubbed up against the back of her sneaker. She stopped to loosen the laces a bit. A ring of pink had already formed she could tell by the light of the street lamp. Fortunately, it hadn't totally blistered yet. Moments later, Emily stopped short to listen. The sound of churning water would normally be soothing, calming even. Not now. "Oh, no, the river!" she exclaimed. "We didn't come this way before, Hayley. We're definitely going in the wrong direction!"

"Uh-oh," Hayley replied. "I think we're lost."

Chapter Fourteen

THE THOUGHT OF BEING trapped in the maze of this unfamiliar town drew Emily's anxiety. She tried to keep her feelings at bay, but fear overtook her and tears drew to her eyes. She wiped them away quickly in an effort to hide her emotions from Hayley. The girl probably already thought her to be a child and crying now in front of her would only confirm it. Images of grand English hedge mazes came to mind from the pictures in her history book. The extravagantly laid out labyrinths—upwards of three miles of pathway in some of them—could be just about impossible to navigate. How long could it take a person to find their way out? The only saving grace now was that she had Hayley with her, plus her cell phone, and she wasn't behind a tall hedge that could obscure everything completely. At least, there were street lights to guide. She reached into her pocket and pulled out her phone. Unfortunately, it was useless as the signal was too weak to make any connection.

"I'm so thirsty," she said, lamenting the fact that she didn't get a bottled water when she had the chance. She cast her gaze down the street, hoping for a 24-hour convenience store or anyplace open at this hour.

"Me, too," echoed Hayley while shifting her hobo bag to the other shoulder. The tinkling sound of something fragile came from inside the bag.

"What's in there?" Emily asked. "Sounds like glass—or something."

"Nothing important." Hayley put a protective hand over the clasp. "Just stuff."

A sense of dread overcame Emily. The commercial district had all but closed for the night. Very few cars—if any—even came down the street.

"I think we'd better go back the other way. This isn't the right direction." Emily turned around and before going more than a few paces, she slowed her gait and then froze.

"Why'd you stop, Em?"

"I-I don't feel right."

"You're sick?"

"No. That guy."

"What guy? Where?"

"Up the block—but, wait—don't look obvious. He just got out," Emily said, eyeing him askance. She remembered the white vehicle passing by them before; it was the one now parked at the corner.

"So? What's the problem? He looks like he's just having a smoke."

"That car looks familiar." Emily hushed her voice. "I think it's been trailing us."

"Em, I think you've been watching too many thrillers."

Emily's nerves tensed. "It might be nothing, but I don't want to walk by him."

Call it instinct, but every cell in her body said to get out of there. If only they hadn't been so conspicuously out in the open—and alone. She kept her eyes fixed and watched him take a step down the sidewalk in their direction. Emily's pulse quickened. "Come on, Hayley." Emily grabbed her friend by the strap of her bag. "Let's go!"

Emily hustled across the street with Hayley at her heels. She led at a clipped pace until the scent of woods and water became prominent again. *This isn't the right way. . .oh, which way to go?* Emily took a gamble and made a right at the corner and scurried down to the next block toward the direction they probably should have been going in the first place.

"Okay. . .wait," Hayley called out.

Emily turned and stopped to catch her breath.

"Damn!"

"You okay?"

"My sandal. The strap came loose."

Emily watched as Hayley fiddled with the sandal and, while still breathing hard, she searched up and down the street. Not seeing anything amiss and no one behind them, she pointed to the left. "I think the campus is this way. Let's just stay in one direction this time and see where it leads us." She hustled down the street, picking up her stride as she went.

"Fine with me. . .ouch, wait up," Hayley cried, attempting to keep up the pace.

"Did you fix it?" Emily called back.

"No, I'll just go barefoot."

"The campus shouldn't be too much farther ahead," Emily said, double-timing her steps. *God, please lead us back safely.*

A couple of blocks later, Emily's frustration turned to hopelessness when the street came to a dead end at a gnarled thicket beside a big trash receptacle. *Now what?* Compounding things was something else. Across the street loomed the same white car that passed them earlier. The despair that draped over her quickly escalated to fear at seeing the figure of a man heading in their direction. The way he walked and that smirk of a smile—more chiseled than warm—gave her the creeps. Why was he wearing sunglasses at night? Emily stood cold in her tracks. Her pulse beat in her ears while her imagination rose into overdrive.

"Need a ride, ladies?" he said in a slightly southern drawl and whipped off his glasses. The look in his eyes—the cold, hard stare—didn't look friendly in the least to Emily. Her throat turned dry and her heart thumped in overtime. A trickle of sweat rolled down her left arm. "Seen you been walking around town without an escort. . .not a good idea." He smirked again.

Emily shot a glance at Hayley, hoping that she sensed the danger, too, as he came closer. After seeing one too many thriller movies, she couldn't walk down a dark, empty alley without thinking someone was following her. Was she paranoid? She didn't care. Either way, her instincts would not betray her; this unsettled feeling deep down was there for a reason. The man stepped closer. He was about fifty feet away now. . .then forty. . .thirty. . .twenty. . . The adrenaline coursing through her veins summoned a nerve she didn't know she owned.

"Run, Hayley!" she shouted and madly bolted across the street. Emily ran blindly, not even daring to turn around. Either Hayley was with her or not, but the chance the man was on her heels would be too scary to find out. Better not even look, though something about him seemed vaguely familiar and she tried to place him. He may or may not have been a bad actor, but now was not the time to find out. While it was hard to tell in the dark, she still wondered if she knew him from somewhere?

Her chest heaved as she sucked up the air she was expending. She kept running. . .past the post office, a funeral home, and then an ivy-covered building before approaching a warehouse. Breathlessly, she scrambled around the building, keeping up the pace of an Olympian athlete. Her athleticism in school, which proved her to be the best eighth-grade short distance runner, came to be a blessing. The image of a roaring lion not far behind harnessed her energy and kept her moving no less swiftly than a fired-up locomotive leaving the station. Her legs—now moving faster than her body could carry them—soon turned rubbery until they could no longer hold her. A moment later, she went down, taking a hard fall on the ground.

"Owww," she cried out in pain as her bare knee met the sharp edge of a semi-buried rock. Blood rushed to the surface and began to trickle down her leg. Hot, sweating, and out of breath, she took the hem of her cotton top and pressed it to her knee to stop the oozing flow. She cringed at the sight of the blood staining the bright white of her T-shirt. While she dabbed her knee, the sound of rushing water beckoned beyond the trees. Though her instincts told her this still wasn't the right direction to get back to the camp, she managed to stand up and press on, bloody knee and all, toward the water.

Security lights on the roof top of a warehouse revealed a clearing in the weedy overgrowth that led to a path through some gnarled trees. She cut through the brush and bramble and stopped short at the edge of a steep river bank. The angle couldn't have been more sheer—practically a 90 degree drop into the water. Behind her rose an odd sounding squall she didn't recognize. Animal or human? She couldn't tell. Panic took another stab, sending a jolt of adrenaline through her limbs.

Far below, the river cascaded tirelessly over rocks and boulders on its way downstream. In the darkness, the water sounded ominously imposing like a waterfall, reminding her of the surging flow of the famous Niagara Falls that had frightened her as a child. Even while holding her father's hand on the sidewalk several blocks away, the power of the roaring water was daunting to her as it caused the sidewalk underneath her feet to quake.

Emily followed the path that eventually led to a footbridge to the other side of the river. In the darkness, her heart trembled—both out of fear that the footbridge might not be stable if she put her weight on it, and also that the strange man wasn't still somewhere behind her and ready to pounce. He couldn't have chased both of them down. What were the odds that he'd chosen her and was lurking somewhere behind? Then a sense of guilt rose. Poor Hailey. He may have gotten a hold of her. Without her sandals, how could the girl have even run at all?

Chapter Fifteen

Faint moon light cast an eerie glow as Emily's paranoia grew. She braced herself and took a tentative step onto the foot bridge. The rickety wood swayed under her weight. She'd been on the same type of bridge before when she'd visited relatives in Montana. The rush of the Kootenai River rapids far below had been daunting enough to take her breath away back then, and midway across the rapids, the bridge shook even more vigorously as others stepped onto it behind her. Their weight shook not only the bridge but her composure as well. What if the wooden slats cracked midway or the rope frayed and snapped? How far down would she drop into the deep, dark river?

The same fear overtook her once again as she trembled alone in the dark. While standing midway with fear gripping down to her bones, Emily spotted a copse of trees a little way down the river jutting out from a tiny island. In the dimness, there was just enough on-shore light to see a boat docked, and she heard the sound of voices floating across the water. She wanted to cry out for help but feared calling attention to herself. Surely, someone could help her to get back to where she belonged. If only someone knew she was there.

****

"What are you doing?" Hayley's words muffled underneath the gag.

"Quiet," he barked.

"Where are you taking me?" She writhed under the constricting cords wrapped around her wrists, struggling to release herself. Her skin chafed against the rough thread. Thankfully, he'd tied them together in front of her body instead of behind it, and her hobo knapsack bag was still attached to her side.

"Tell me where!" she screamed.

"If I wanted ya t'know, I'd a told ya," he snapped and slammed the trunk lid down on top of her.

In the darkness, Hayley laid in shock. Her heart beat wildly and her head throbbed. Tears came silently as sweat tricked down her neck. In the heat of the stifling trunk, she could barely breathe.

****

Emily stepped off the other side of the rickety bridge, relieved that she made it across. Despite the ache in her knee, she pressed on and followed the way along the stony bank in the direction of the island. The little oasis in the midst of the river beckoned as tiny lights winked through the gently swaying trees. *A campsite?* Her highly fueled anxiety eased back a notch at the hopeful thought someone on the island could lend help. The only problem was getting their attention. Would she have to swim across the river to get it?

One tentative step at a time, she made her way down the steep embankment. Clinging to rocks and boulders, one after the other, she clambered across the rough terrain through the semi-darkness. A giant boulder jutting out from the bank served for support. She grabbed onto it with both hands.

"Hello!" she called out. "Hey!" Nothing called back but the chirp of crickets.

The rushing water gurgled and churned louder as she approached the river. Who knew what danger was possibly there in the depths of the murky water? Even by daylight, rivers could harbor menacing things—snakes, biting reptiles—and she'd freak out if one ever came close. Could she even make it all the way to the island? Emily's thoughts churned as the water's edge grew closer. She flinched as mud oozed into her sneakers. Then the ominous sound of something thrashing in the woods at the top of the bank rattled her once more. She had to move fast. Knowing her cell phone would be useless once it got wet, she pulled it out of her back pocket and set it on one of the boulders as far up as she could reach. She hated the idea of leaving it behind, but there was no other choice. At the startling sound of whatever it thrashed louder, she twisted around to face the water and swiftly lost her footing. In a second, she was airborne and, moments later, landed squarely on a half-submerged rock. The last thing she heard was the thud of her head followed by immense pain and then blackness.

****

Hayley's mind spun with all that was happening in the struggle with her captor. Trapped inside the car was a living nightmare. Unfortunately, her hobo satchel didn't knock him out when she swung it at his head earlier on the dead-end street, but it lent an advantage—at least for Emily, who was able to get away and run—somewhere? Hayley was glad one of them escaped. Lucky for Emily, but Hayley wished it had been herself. She cursed herself for not wearing sneakers, like Emily. Her bare feet were sore and scraped from all of the debris she stepped on after her sandal strap broke, and her body trembled and sweat from head to toe from the intense heat.

Hayley tried all she could to unbind her wrists and chew the rag pressed across her mouth but to no avail. Wrestling with the constraints only made her sweat more. Exhausted from the struggle, she groaned and begrudgingly resigned herself to the confines of the dirty trunk floor as her captor hightailed the car out of town. His erratic driving tossed and shuffled her for a while until the car eventually seemed to be going in a straight line. Now, the car was on a highway or some other road without stop signs or traffic lights and traveling at a good rate of speed. The bumping and rattling sounds along with the whine of the tires on asphalt hissed in her ears.

Hayley laid trembling in pitch blackness. The cruel reality of her hopeless predicament weighed her down both physically and mentally, leaving her feeling little more than a living mummy trapped in a cave, bound and wrapped for life. Cognizant of her own breathing, she feared the next inhalation might be her last. In-and-out, she pictured her lungs taking in and giving away the precious air that kept her alive. How much was left inside this putrid old car trunk? Her breathing came in shallow pants. Fear of not getting enough oxygen kept her in a heightened state of anxiety. Where her fear left off, her frustration and anger at the situation took over. She fought to unleash herself. Twisting and tugging at the bands on her wrists left them sore and near bleeding. She got one wrist partially loose but at the expense of shredding her skin any further, she gave up.

Still bound and gagged, her anxious thoughts weighed her down. Would she die or be raped. . .or both? Every imaginable evil thing that could happen to a girl in her situation—one just as frighting as the next—popped into her head. As each minute passed, Hayley resented the ogre of a man who'd put her in this vulnerable state. *Damn this creep!* But she brought it on herself, she knew. Going to the Stacks wasn't her best idea, but staying at the campus eating the cafeteria food and being forced to be in bed by nine was a total turn-off.

For the next hour or so, Hayley lay awake listening to the whirring of moving tires as the car sped down the roadway. Thoughts about the hockey camp once again came to mind. How it irked her that her mother sent her away in the first place. Though right now, the camp with all of its annoyances was a welcome oasis compared to the despair of her present condition.

After a long time of smooth going, the car began to rock and sway, sending her rolling around until the vehicle eventually came to a stop. She perked up and strained to hear who or what was outside the car. She struggled with the binding on her left wrist and fought with all the strength she could muster by using her fingers and teeth. At this point, possibly loosening or even losing a front tooth took a back seat to her resolve to be free. She was determined to get out of the restraints. While tugging and biting, another sound came—the sound of the door to the gas tank popping open. Her desperation sank to a new low at the thought of him having to refuel and wondering just how far away was he taking her? Just as the fuel entered into the tank, she noticed a pale sliver of light. She scooted over and saw the light was coming from *outside* the car. He'd accidentally popped open the back trunk!

Hayley's mind spun with options. She wanted to push the trunk up with her head or even her elbow and scream for attention, but if he were standing there at the fuel tank, he'd be sure to catch her. He'd either slap her down to shut her up or slam the lid back down in a nanosecond. Shivering now as adrenaline coursed through her, she listened as the fuel poured into the tank. Then it stopped. He put the nozzle back and recapped the fuel tank. It was now or never to make her move.

With her heart in her throat, she gathered the courage to be her own hero. Every second counted for her to push her way out. Fortunately, the wrist ties were frayed enough that she was able to pull one wrist free. Still bound at the ankles, she wouldn't be able to hop out and run, but she'd make it her goal to get out any way she could. Hayley's pulse thrummed into overdrive. With one hand free, she slowly lifted the trunk lid a fraction. There was no way to see him at this angle as she carefully peered through the slim line created by the open lid. The fluorescent lights at the gas station assaulted her eyes and it took a moment to see before her eyes adjusted. The gas pumps directly behind the vehicle were void of any cars and the station was apparently self-serve only. Her heart sank. No one to signal or call to. *What time was it?* Still without a clue and with no one to help her, she was on her own.

The car bounced as he got back inside and turned on the ignition. In a second, the engine revved and he was off. Hayley's body still surged with adrenaline. As the car maneuvered out of the gas station and onto the highway, she pressed her free hand to the lid.

Hanging onto the edge of the car in a crouched position with her ankles still tied, she sprung up to attempt a daring leap out of the moving vehicle. Rolling down the embankment of the highway's on-ramp, the last thing she saw was a set of headlights barreling toward her.

Chapter Sixteen

June 10

8:04 a.m.

"Good morning, ladies," Coach Kearns called to the girls while walking onto the field holding a case of bottled water. She plopped it down by the bleachers, adjusted her visor, and wiped her face with the towel from around her neck. "Hope everyone is ready for today's exercises. Today, we'll be doing some drills—passing, dribbling. . .so, let's line up and get started."

After the initial warm up exercises, the coach picked up her clipboard from the bench. "Okay, first team, you're up." She studied the clip board and called out the players. "Madison, Kelly, Gracie, Jordanna, Hayley, Emily, Ashley, Sarah, Arden, Kaitlyn, and Taylor." The girls hustled onto the field with sticks and mouth guards in hand. The coach pushed her visor up as though perplexed. "Where's Hayley and Emily?" She glanced around the field. "Has anyone seen them this morning?"

"They weren't in the dining hall for dinner last night," one of the girls said.

"I didn't see them at breakfast," another replied.

Coach Kearns' frown drew lines between her eyes. "Well, seems we don't have Hayley or Emily with us this morning. All right, let's see. How about we substitute Jenna and Liv. You two will play right and left wing today." She placed her clipboard down on the bleachers and shouted, "Okay, girls, ready?" and blew her whistle.

****

At the end of practice, Taylor ran up to Coach Kearns as she headed off the field and toward the main office on campus.

"Coach!" Taylor stood, pink-faced and sweating, trying to catch her breath.

"Yes? Nice save, by the way, on that corner. . .good stick work," the coach commended. "You wanted to say something?"

"Yeah. I. . .um. . .thought you should know," Taylor began. "I'm pretty sure Emily and Hayley went somewhere last night."

"Oh?"

"I don't think they came back, either. I didn't see them in the bathroom or at breakfast in the dining hall this morning."

"Oh, this isn't good," the coach said with a frown.

"Emily asked me if I wanted to go with her and Hayley somewhere. . .but I didn't want to."

"Do you know where they went?"

Taylor shook her head. "The Max. . .or something like that."

"The Max?" Coach Kearns mouthed the words as though conjuring up its recognition.

"Hmmm. . .I've never heard of it. Is it a restaurant?"

Taylor shrugged.

"Max. . .max?" the coach repeated. "Wait, could it possibly be the *Stacks?*"

"Um, yeah. I think that might be it."

"Well, I'll need to report this," the coach replied. "Thanks for letting me know, Taylor."

Chapter Seventeen

SARAH DROVE UP ONTO Cindy's driveway and rolled down the window. She grinned broadly and called out to Cindy, who stood waiting at the top of the hill, "Ready to check out the new digs?"

"Hey, there!" Cindy ambled her hefty body toward the red Subaru. "*Your* new digs?" She smiled stepping in and strapping on her seatbelt.

"From your lips to God's ears." Sarah pointed her index finger up. "I don't want to jinx it. So, I'm not saying anything more."

"Bah. So, what's the worst that can happen?"

Sarah shrugged. "I might not get that seller's assist thing."

"You know, hon, we'd lend you the money—that is, if we had it. It's pretty much hand-to-mouth for Joe and me these days."

Sarah waved her hand dismissively. "Oh, Cindy, I wouldn't think of ever asking you. Please don't feel bad."

"Well, I'd just love to help if I could. I mean—"

"I know. You're very sweet to offer, but if it's meant to be, it will be."

"I just know how much you hate the rent thing."

"Got that right."

Sarah drove for a few miles through town. At the upcoming intersection, she turned right and drove up the hill. "Okay, it should be coming up on the left. . .right around the corner just past the golf course."

Soon the condos came into view. Sarah's stomach danced. The high-rise condominiums, surrounded by a stunning landscape of smartly clustered shrubs and flowering trees along neatly trimmed hedges, towered above the trees. A glistening pond sat at the edge of the property.

"Wow, not too shabby," Cindy commented as she took in the property.

Sarah's heart lifted as she pulled into a parking space and turned off the engine. *Just hope it's in the cards for me.*

****

"And this is the two-bedroom," the real estate agent explained as she opened the door to the unit. Bright sunlight flooded the over-sized living room and bounced off the shiny hardwood floor. "Lots of natural light," she commented and moved on to the next room.

"Nice view," Sarah said of the panorama that included the golf course.

"Yes, it is lovely. You're right above the golf course," Evelyn replied. "Play golf, do you?"

"No, no." Sarah smiled.

"Yes, well, your maintenance fee includes membership to the pool, tennis courts, the gym and sauna facilities. Tee time is extra. And with an open floor plan"—the agent tutted about the unit—"you can do a lot space-wise. Unless a three-bedroom is a better fit?"

"A two-bedroom would be ideal," Sarah began. "It's just me and my daughter."

The agent prattled on about the amenities as she breezed through the unit. She pointed out the special features of the bath-room with its jacuzzi and stall shower as well as the ice maker in the refrigerator and state-of-the-art windows.

As Sarah walked through the rooms, she pictured what her furniture would look like inside the well-appointed unit. Oak floors, new model fixtures, a contemporary kitchen that reflected cutting-edge design, so unlike her present one with the bland, outdated color scheme and cut marks in the Formica countertops that set her teeth on edge every time she noticed them. Everything about the condo impressed her and would suit her needs perfectly. The only issue now was money.

"Would you like to see the rest of the building? I can give you the grand tour?" Evelyn lent a professional smile.

"Sure," Sarah replied, glancing at Cindy, who nodded in agreement.

On the way out the door, Sarah's cell rang. "Just a sec,"—she held up a finger—"be with you in a moment."

"Mrs. Harding?" the voice chirped through the phone.

"Yes, speaking."

"This is Maddie Blackwood, director of Lebanon Valley Hockey Camp."

A sudden weight descended on Sarah's chest. For a moment, she couldn't breathe. *Why was she calling? This couldn't be good news.*

"I wanted to share some serious information with you."

Silence.

"Ms. Harding? Are you still there?"

"Yes-yes, I'm still here," Sarah managed to say.

"I'm sorry to be calling you like this. And I'm not sure of all of the details at this point, but I'm reaching out to let you know there's a problem here—"

"Wha-what is it?"

"There's a serious situation up here at the camp."

Sarah's stomach cinched.

"We have some news—"

"News? What kind of news?"

"There are a couple of girls missing. "One of the girls is Hayley Benson."

"Hayley? Oh, no!"

"Yes, and the other girl missing. . .I'm so sorry to say. . .is your daughter."

Chapter Eighteen

"SARAH, WHAT'S WRONG, HON?"

"Emily," she sobbed to Cindy. "They can't find her." She dissolved into a puddle of tears.

"What?"

"The camp. . .she's missing." Her whole body trembled. "The lady said they can't find her nor Hayley." Sarah wiped her eyes. "I'm going up there."

"To Bethlehem? When. . .now?"

"Right now." Sarah shoved her phone back into her purse and double-timed her steps out the door.

"But. . .but you're too upset. You're shaking for crying out loud, Sarah. Let the authorities handle it."

"No," Sarah said. "I can't just sit around, Cindy. You know me." She rummaged in her pocket and pulled out her car key. "I need to find her."

Outside in the hallway, Evelyn stood by the elevators. "Oh, just in time," she announced. "We'll start on the ground floor. I'll show you the inside amenities first, and then we can. . ." Her face fell. "Is everything okay ladies?"

"Actually, no," Sarah spoke up. "I have an emergency."

"Oh, dear. I'm so sorry." She folded her arms across her chest as the elevator door opened. "Well, not a problem. We can always take the tour at another time."

Sarah dabbed her eyes with the back of her hand. "Thanks for understanding." As thrilling as it would be to see everything luxury condo living could offer, right now the only vision Sarah needed was to see her daughter's face.

The three women boarded the waiting elevator, and Sarah pressed the button for the ground floor. When the elevator door opened, Sarah made a beeline for the parking lot with Cindy hastening to keep up. As she unlocked the car, Sarah's mind spun. She practically willed the car up toward the camp in upstate Pennsylvania, but off the top of her head, she couldn't remember the address.

"Great," she exclaimed, banging both hands on the steering wheel. "I don't even know how to get there!"

"Where's the camp. . .what's the name?" Cindy said as she climbed in.

"Um, it's Lebanon Valley something. . .hosted by Moravian University."

The paperwork for the tuition with the letterhead was on her desk back home. Her anxiety mounting at this point, she pulled out her cell phone and began to search for the name of the camp.

"I'll go with you. You can't go alone."

"No, no, I'll be fine." Sarah continued scrolling. "Ah, here it is."

"What is it?" Cindy asked. "I'll plug it in. Is the GPS in the glove compartment?"

"Yes, it's right there. Okay, it's 1200 Main Street, Bethlehem."

"Hold on." Cindy pulled out the black box and typed the information into the GPS. "Okay, it's in."

Sarah backed out of the condo's parking lot as the GPS voice began communicating.

"Thanks for coming with me today," Sarah said. "But I'd better drive up there myself."

"What? No moral support?" Cindy made a face.

"Thanks, I appreciate it, Cin, but I'm just too rattled right now. I wouldn't be good company, you know? And I don't want to burden you or anyone with this."

"But—"

"No buts. I'll be fine."

Cindy sighed. "Promise?"

"Promise."

On the way back to drop off Cindy, Sarah's mind flew in a dozen directions. Her thoughts swirled as anxiety ripped her heart. *Emily, where are you? What happened?* Sarah's heart bled as her thoughts turned into prayers the rest of the way to Cindy's house. As Sarah pulled up, Cindy said, "Well, I'll be calling you in an hour to see if you've gotten there safely." She opened the door and got out. "Keep me abreast of your progress," she said through the open window.

"I will." Sarah revved the motor, impatiently.

"Go, honey. . .I'll be praying they find her."

"Appreciate it, Cin, thanks," she called out the window. Sarah turned at the next intersection and made her way through the back streets to I-476. From there, she followed the signs to the Northeast Extension for the hour-long ride to the campus in Bethlehem. Her heartbeat ticked a notch higher as she drove a bit faster than normal while she fiddled with the radio to hear the latest traffic conditions. Once on the Extension, the road appeared clear and up-to-speed in both directions. She pressed her foot to the pedal. The ache in her heart over her missing daughter pressed in like a dull knife.

Chapter Nineteen

THE ROSEWOOD CAFÉ HUMMED with an understated vibe. Soft lighting and the nostalgia of Big Band era tunes gently piped in lent to the taste of an older crowd blended with a few millennials.

"Just a sec," Cindy called out as she raised her index finger while maneuvering a cart topped with entrees to a table of locals from the insurance company across the street. "Here you go, fellas." Cindy handed each of them plates of hot roast beef sandwiches, sides of sauerkraut, French fries, and mugs of draft beer. She wheeled the cart back and brought a carafe of coffee to another regular, a retired oil worker, who came into the café every weekday precisely at 12:05 p.m. and stayed for an hour for as long as Cindy could remember. "Anything else, Ches?"

"Nope, I'm good, hon." He plopped down cash on top of the check lying on the table with a generous tip for Cindy included, as always.

"Sounds good. Have a lovely. . .see you tomorrow," she replied.

Cindy tended to another patron signaling for his check, and then went back to the kitchen. On the way, she caught a glimpse of a familiar customer coming into the café.

"Nicky!" she greeted him with a smile. "Long time no see. Where ya been, guy?"

"Been around," he said with a half-shrug.

"Well, I musta missed ya. What'll it be today, your usual?"

"Sounds about right," he said with a nod and sat himself at the end of the counter.

She scribbled his order down and gave it to the man behind the counter before reaching into the ice bin for a bottled water. She felt Nick's pain having understood the hurt of what broken love can do and gave him a sympathetic smile. He didn't seem to notice. A few minutes later she placed his sandwich in front of him along with the bottle and a glass. While he ate, she hesitated whether to bring up Sarah. Though later, even before he finished, she couldn't wait any longer. "Did you hear about Sarah?"

"*My* Sarah—um, well, not my—"

"I know, I heard. So sorry about what happened between you guys."

Nick shrugged again. "It is what it is. Crap happens, right?"

"Nicky, I wanted you to know something that happened—to Sarah—well, to her daughter, that is."

"Emily?"

Cindy nodded. "She's missing."

"Missing"—his face folded—"as in a runaway?"

"Oh, I doubt it, no. . .well, no one knows, really. It only just happened."

Nick sat up a bit straighter and put the last bit of the sandwich down on the plate.

"The camp director just notified her. We were together when she got the call."

"Where's the camp?"

"Bethlehem. It's a hockey camp up at Moravian University."

Nick's eyes grew large as he stared at the TV hanging above the bar. Cindy followed his gaze and caught a glimpse of the faces of two young teenage girls flash across the screen.

"That's Emily!" Cindy cried, pointing to the TV. "And another girl. . .is she missing, too? Did they find them or. . .?" she questioned as she hustled over to the remote lying on the counter and used it to turn the sound up just as the segment ended. "Oh, for crying out loud. I hope they were found!"

Nick stood up and pulled out his wallet. He plopped down two bills. "Keep the rest, Cindy. . .gotta run."

"You're in a hurry," she said, collecting the cash. "You working today?"

He bolted for the door and with a wave called back, "Could say that, yeah."

Nick hopped into his truck and immediately Googled the address for Moravian University. In a matter of minutes, the GPS map lasered in on the best route to Bethlehem. He stared at the screen. *What am I doing? Is this a fool's mission? She could be anywhere by now.* He didn't know how he'd go about finding Emily in that big town. He only knew that he wanted to find her—needed to find her safe and alive. It was more than just being a hero; he'd do anything to make amends for any undoing between himself and Sarah. What he did wrong to get her upset enough to call it quits on their relationship was anyone's guess. She complained a lot about his work and his smoking, but it couldn't have been just that. When she dropped the bomb on him, he couldn't sleep or eat for days. Meantime, she'd given him the incentive to quit his life-long smoking habit. While he hadn't succeeded yet, he was trying. The break-up was good for one thing, at least. He didn't owe her a thing, really. So, why was he so determined to be her hero now?

Several miles into the trip, traffic began to slow on the Northeast Extension until a mile before Quakertown where it came to a complete stop. He drummed his fingers on the wheel and steeled his eyes ahead toward a sea of brake lights before picking up his phone and pressing speed dial.

"Traffic Center, Tony speaking."

"Tony, this is Nick Durham," he said to Tony Nixon, Director of Operations at Metro Traffic in Philadelphia.

"Officer Durham. Been awhile. What's the good word?"

"Yeah, I thought you could tell me." He half-heartedly chuckled under his breath. "I'm on the Northeast Extension just past Lansdale. . .almost to Quakertown. Need to get to Bethlehem."

"Oh, boy. Then you've got a problem, sir."

Nick cursed under his breath. "What's the problem?"

"Well, the road's been closed for about an hour just below Quakertown. Overturned tractor trailer and a Subaru, I think. Squashed it like a bug."

Nick's insides twisted at the image now plastered in his mind. *Subaru?*

"Happen to know what color it was?"

"Ahhh, let's see. Lemme check. . .um. . .unfortunately, we don't have a camera on the Northeast Extension, or I could zoom in on it, but pilot 402 was recently up there and. . .wait. . .ok, yeah, let me check. Hold on, be right with you."

After sitting in bumper-to-bumper traffic, Nick's lack of patience got the better of him. He fussed and fidgeted in the seat, more than annoyed at his predicament. Rushing to aid his former girlfriend to win her over was a losing man's game. Yet here he was. He silently cursed his bad luck.

"Sorry to hold you, Officer. You still there?"

"Yeah, Tony. I'm here."

"Okay . . . I was told it was a red Subaru and an 18-wheeler. Had to send a Medevac unit to the scene." Nick's heart sank at the thought the car may have belonged to Sarah. "So, that's the latest. . ." Nick sat stunned to hear the news. "Officer?"

"Yeah, Tony. Thanks for your trouble."

"No problem, sir. The lanes just re-opened, so the backlog should be clearing out, but it could be a while before you're up-to-speed. Hang in there."

"Okay, thanks for the information. You guys do some great work."

"It's just our job, sir, but thanks."

Gripping the wheel as though willing the car to fly up and over the back-up, Nick gritted his teeth. Maybe this was just some kind of heavenly signal to leave well enough alone. The relationship was over. There were other women; Sarah Harding wasn't the only beauty left in the world. He considered turning around and just giving up the chase. This was what it was. A chase. Although he cared deeply for her—whether she survived the accident or not was important to him—who's to say what would come of it?

What was the use in attempting to get involved with Sarah again? It would just lead to more heartache.

As Nick sat waiting in the backed-up traffic, he noticed a layer of dust piled up on the dashboard. He reached inside the over-stuffed glove compartment for a tissue to wipe the surface clean. With traffic at a standstill, he used the time to better organize the contents and pulled out old receipts and papers that he should have tossed by now. After tidying up the side console as well, he then reached under the driver's seat where he kept a pack of ciga-rettes. With everything going on in his life, the stress he bore right now lent a longing for the calming effects of tobacco. He pulled out a lone cigarette and inhaled the inside of the empty package. With a sense of guilt, he reached for the lighter and lit up. The savory essence of the smokey warmth inside his mouth tasted delicious. In less than sixty seconds, the cigarette lowered his stress. As he let the smoke seep out from his lips, a measure of regret crept in. He fought the subtle urge to flick the rest of the cigarette out the window but lost the battle.

Up ahead, the red tail lights of the car in front disappeared, signaling traffic was moving. *Thank God!* Nick pressed the ac-celerator fast and hard to make up for lost time. He couldn't go fast enough and was tempted to put on the siren. Even though he wasn't clocked in for duty, this was police work—official or not.

Chapter Twenty

"I've begun the Hydromorphone," the onboard nurse announced as she checked the IV.

"The patient is secure, sir." The paramedic turned to the pilot. "Any cautions?"

"No cautions. All clear. All instruments in the green."

"Fuel?"

"One hour thirty minutes."

"Two to fly."

"Okay."

"We're in flight mode. EMS-371 is lifting. Four souls on board. Inbound for Lehigh Valley."

The technician studied Sarah as she lay unconscious on the gurney. "Patient looks to be in her mid-to-late thirties. Doesn't look good."

****

"Emergency trauma two," the lead nurse at Lehigh Valley hospital called out as the EMS team bolted through the double doors.

"Left ac joint and a 14-gauge on her left hand," the paramedic announced. "With 80 systolic. A lotta blood lost, I'm afraid."

"Pain meds administered?" the lead nurse questioned.

"Hydromorphone—2.5mL."

"Okay, got it. Any family on board?"

"No, no one," the 2nd paramedic replied. "No wedding ring, either."

The emergency trauma team got into action like a choreographed dance routine. One assistant placed a chest tube while the other drew blood.

"Her breathing is decreased," the lead surgeon announced. "We'll probably need a CT but not until her vitals are steady. Keep me posted." The doctor continued to examine Sarah. "Doesn't appear to be any brain hemorrhage but you never know; we'll need to keep a close eye out."

"Doctor, her vitals are steady."

"Airway?"

"All open, sir."

"Get a scan."

Chapter Twenty-one
Earlier that morning
6:31 a.m.

THE SUN CREPT OVER the Lehigh River as Emily opened her eyes. In the muggy heat, she cringed at seeing her fingers so puckered—the skin having shriveled overnight from lying in the water. Mud soaked through her wet clothes as a numbing cold pressed in. *Where am I?* It took a moment to process what happened. The back of her head ached. She winced at the pain. Touching her head now, the lump felt like a walnut. She strained to sit up but was too weak. As the sun peaked out through the trees lining the river, Emily tried, once more, to rise up out of the mud-soaked water where she'd been half-submerged. With one elbow on the muddy ground, combined with all the effort she could muster, she finally propped herself up. Despite the pleasant early morning warmth of June, she shivered in her wet clothes.

Nearly faint with dizziness, Emily took her first step out of the lapping river and then another. That was as far as she could go. She plopped down on the embankment. After a minute, she slowly turned her head to look up and down the river. *Would there be anyone to help?* She laid back down on the ground. Her mind reeled back to the hours before when she ran away from the strange man on the street. *Did he catch Hayley or did she escape?*

Emily struggled to move again. A dull ache throbbed in her head and a foggy veil shrouded her vision. She continued to fight with every ounce of energy in her weakened state to move off the river bank and onto dry ground. Through the fog that hung over her, the world looked dim and cloudy as though the aperture setting on a camera lens was smudged. A dusty sun hovered through the trees, and the grayish river barely sparkled in the morning light. Cold and frightened, she perked up at the sound of faint voices coming from down the river. *Someone to the rescue?*

"Help!" she cried out on the edge of the bank as a boat cruised by. In vain, she called again, but her voice barely made a dent in the atmosphere of happily chirping birds amid the rushing water. Apparently, the fisherman on board were too distracted with finding fish than picking up her distress call. Disheartened, she waved one hand in the air as far as she could reach upwards in an effort to send a signal. By the time she raised it, the boat had already drifted off into the shadows.

Chapter Twenty-two

AN ORDERLY WHEELED SARAH into room #408 at Lehigh Valley Hospital, her life being spared miraculously from the tragic car accident where she suffered injuries that left her with a broken arm, a concussion, and internal bleeding. Her race with time caused the collision with an 18-wheeler that ended up pinning and totally crushing her car on the Northeast Extension. All lanes were shut down for an hour while they cleared the debris to make room for the Medevac helicopter to land and transport the injured.

"Is there anything more you need right now?" the nurse asked.

"I need. . .to find. . .my daughter." Sarah barely managed to get the words out.

The nurse gave Sarah a kind smile and patted the bedsheet. "Was she in the car with you?"

"No. . .no, she's at camp" *Or was.*

The nurse spoke again, but Sarah couldn't make out her words. The room spun and turned dark. She then fell asleep under the heavy sedation. While sedated, she envisioned Emily caught in a well, and the firemen who came to rescue her could only hear her calling from deep below. No one could see her.

When Sarah awoke, reality gobsmacked her once more. *Oh, God, my daughter. . .where are you?* Later while lying in bed, Sarah's desperation to find Emily weighed on her mind as though this were all a bad dream. Between the pain killers flushed into her veins through the IV along with the oral meds, Sarah didn't know whether she was coming or going, and the nightmare wouldn't end. The image of the accident came to the forefront as flashes of the roadway appeared, taunting her. She vividly recalled how she managed to squeeze between the concrete barrier wall to her right and the massive 18-wheeler truck to her left in the adjacent lane. A chill ran through her even though the hospital's bed clothes kept the room warm as toast. Her thinking was that if she could make it past the truck—she needed to take every advantage to make haste to find her daughter—it would have been a good thing. Pressing the accelerator, Sarah tensed up as her eyes darted between the wall and the huge trucks tires. . .back and forth. . .wall. . .tires. . .wall. . .tires. . .she kept a steady eye, willing herself to remain safely in between. Thankfully, it wasn't raining and the roadway was dry. She gunned down again, the speedometer reading 70. . .75. . .80. . .Still sandwiched between the wall and the truck, Sarah held her breath until the moment of shock hit. She made a drastic error in judgment and realized she was in trouble when the truck's tires slowly crossed the white lines. The truck was drifting into her lane! The sound of crunching metal impacting forcefully was the last she heard.

****

"She's lucky to be alive," the nurse said quietly to Cindy Holden, who stood in the doorway, as they observed Sarah.

Cindy frowned. "From what I heard, it's a miracle that truck didn't crush her car to bits."

They waited quietly at the door while the doctor stood at Sarah's bedside.

"Sarah. . .Sarah? Sarah, it's Dr. Byron."

Sarah's eyes opened. "Doctor," she said, weakly. "Doctor, I need—I need to find—" She fought the confines of the sheet and started peeling back the tape on her wrist.

"No, no. . .you need that. Take it easy." He reached out to stop her from going any further. "You have some serious internal injuries. We're keeping our eye on things—a close eye. So, please know that you're in good hands."

Sarah lay back down with an audible sigh. "But you don't understand. . .I need to find my daughter."

The doctor gave a puzzled look.

"Doctor?" Cindy stepped closer to the bed. "Hi, Doctor. I'm Sarah's friend, Cindy. You see, my friend's daughter is—well, we don't know right now. She's missing. That's the problem. Sarah's worried to death—we all are."

The doctor's face turned pensive. "I see. That's awful." He turned to Sarah. "I'm sorry for your predicament, Sarah. I know it's hard. But at least for now, you'll need to let the authorities take care of finding your daughter." He put his hand on her shoulder. "You have my complete sympathy, but in your condition, you need to stay in bed. If not, you won't be much good to anyone."

****

Over an hour into the drive, Nick barreled up the Northeast Extension. A quarter mile or so before the exit, hazmat crews were still clearing the debris from the earlier accident. Broken glass and metal remnants of twisted automobile parts lay strewn to the side. He strained to see any evidence of Sarah's car. Maybe Tony had gotten the model wrong and it wasn't her car after all? A car identified as a red Subaru could have been maroon or even rust colored. Was it dark red or cherry? After being scraped and knocked about in an accident, who knew, really, the actual color. Maybe the investigator had been color blind? Desperate to paint the situation less onerous, Nick tried to reason a way out of believing she'd been injured in an accident, especially one where there was a need for a helicopter's assistance.

Nick took the Lehigh Valley exit and made his way to I-78. Entering the town of Bethlehem, he saw signs for Moravian University and eventually wound up on the campus. *Okay, now what to do? Go to the campus police or the official police?* He had no idea where to find any information on Emily or the hockey camp.

"Excuse me," he called out the open window while slowing to a stop in front of a group of girls at the corner of Main and Market streets. "I'm looking for the campus's main office?"

A blonde-haired girl stood out from the pack and pointed ahead. "It's up ahead a few blocks in Colonial Hall. . .it's a stone building."

Nick waved his thanks and resumed speed. A minute later, the stone building appeared just as she said, and he pulled up to park. In the parking lot sat a blue and white police SUV, and a man in a dark blue shirt sat at the wheel. They locked eyes and the officer lowered the window as Nick approached. He flashed his badge.

"Hey, there. I'm Nick Durham, Plymouth police, Montgomery County."

"Hello, officer," the young man replied with an upward nod.

"Yeah, I'm looking to check on the case of the missing girls. . .Emily Harding and another girl."

"The missing girls from Moravian?"

"Yeah, well, they're not students. They're enrolled in the summer hockey camp for girls."

"Oh, okay. . .yeah. I heard something about missing kids. I'm sure the Bethlehem police are handling it."

"Ah, so you're not with the unit?"

"We're just campus police, sir."

"Got it, okay. Is the Bethlehem precinct nearby, or, better yet, do you have their phone number?"

"Should be here, somewhere." the young man said. "Hold on a sec. Should be. . .okay, here it is." He scribbled it down on a piece of paper and handed it to Nick. "Here you go. Good luck."

Chapter Twenty-three

"THE GIRLS WERE LAST seen at the Stacks," Officer Earl Jamison explained to the HRD Cadaver K-9 unit. "The search will take place at the entrance just off of Founders Way and that will include a 10-mile radius in the area between Fountain Hill and Wind Creek with an emphasis on the downtown district between Hayes and Wyandotte. Any questions?"

"What's the status come nightfall?" asked one of the men in the unit.

"We'll cross that bridge when it comes, lieutenant."

"Copy, sir."

"So, we'll canvas the river as well. All of the facts we know are that the girls apparently walked from the campus on foot and left to go back the same way. You each have a map of the area. We'll go as far as the bridge up toward the entrance at Founders Way and throughout the lower end. Follow all of the rules and protocols; you know what they are. Make sure you make note of any additional procedure you use. You can use the ICS-214 form." He looked down at his clipboard. "Anything else, gentlemen?"

"Any other units with us or on stand-by?" the lead agent inquired.

"We're working on that right now. We've made a call to Allentown and Hanover. All my staff is extended as far as we can go. We can use all the help we can get."

All seven men on the HRD team stood silently with their dogs by their sides.

"Okay, if there are no more questions, I'll be in touch by radio. Good luck to all of you."

Nick watched from his car while the K-9 team dispersed and then approached.

"Officer,"—Nick extended his hand—"I'm Sergeant Detective Nick Durham, Plymouth police, Montgomery County."

Officer Jamison's eyebrows raised, "Pleased to make your acquaintance."

"I'm here to help out—if you need another set of eyes. I've got a vested interest in finding the girls—particularly, Emily Harding."

"How's that?"

"Well, she's the daughter of my old girl—well. . .someone I used to know."

Officer Jamison looked intently at him and then gave a sideways grin.

"I've got a soft spot for her, and when I heard. . ." He shrugged and shoved his hands in his pockets.

"Yep, terrible situation for these girls."

Nick rubbed his nose. "You said they were at the Stacks, earlier?"

Officer Jamison nodded. "Got so many citing calls so far, but it's still a crapshoot for sure."

"What's the Stacks?"

"The entertainment center they made out of the old Bethlehem Steel plant." He signaled the direction behind him.

Nick stared down the street where people mingled at outdoor dining tables and milled in and out of boutiques, all oblivious to the situation at hand. His heart sank at what could have been with Sarah vs. his present reality. In the warmth of the gorgeous summer day, he watched a couple sitting at one of the outdoor cafés and pictured himself with Sarah sitting in their place. . .her reddish-brown hair gleaming in the sun. . .a margarita in her hand as she laughed at one of his lame jokes. The image of her lingered in his head. A moment later, he realized there was zero time for daydreaming. His mission now was all about Emily. He was determined to find the girl. Thoughts of Sarah only crystallized his resolve.

"Yeah, okay. You're welcome to join the search party if you want. You can ride with me to the bridge." Officer Jamison said.

Nick snapped out of his reverie and glanced up at him.

"I said, you can ride along in my car if you want," Officer Jamison repeated.

"Oh, yeah, sounds good, thanks. Okay to leave my car here?"

"It'll be fine, but you'll need a placard. Hold on, I've got one."

Nick's adrenaline kicked in. He hadn't been on a search-and-rescue team in a while. At the same time, Tony's words lingered in his head about the totaled red Subaru. He was desperate to know who had been at the wheel and couldn't shake the feeling it might have been Sarah. Between Emily's disappearance and Sarah's possible injuries or even death, the uncertainty of things tore his heart.

Officer Jamison handed Nick the placard for the dashboard. He put it in his car and then got into the officer's sedan to begin the adventure he desperately wanted. Whether Sarah was his girl or not, he longed to be her hero. His feelings for her still left him hollowed like a punch to the gut. He so wanted to reach out and call, and he struggled with the idea, but his pride said, *no, just find Emily.*

✶✶✶✶

A half-dozing Sarah sensed someone in the room, and she slowly opened her eyes. Dr. Byron stood at the foot of the bed. Unable to read his face, she wondered why he was there? Good news. . .bad news? She tried to speak, but all that came out was a garbled litter of words in her ears.

"I understand you're in pain, Sarah. I'm so sorry. But we know of a solution. We've taken a look at the CAT and MRI scans. Seems like the reason for situation is that your spleen was injured pretty badly in your car accident. We're considering whether it best to be repaired or removed. Either way, it should be done asap."

CHAPTER TWENTY-THREE

Sarah nodded slowly.

"And don't worry, you'll be in good hands." He gave her a professional smile behind his steepled fingers. "If you have any questions, please feel free to ask, and when you're ready, we'll need you to sign the consent form, of course."

"Whatever will help me, doctor, thanks."

The much-needed operation was way down on her list of priorities right now. All that Sarah could think of amid her foggy brain was her daughter and the girl's whereabouts. *Lord, please keep her safe.* It was all she wanted to know. As though her child's very life would be all the sustenance she would need to get better. No medication could serve a better outcome.

As the doctor exited the room, Cindy walked in. Sarah felt a bit of strength easing into her body at the sight of her friend.

"I've got to find her, Cindy," Sarah said on the verge of tears. "Has there been any word?"

"Not yet, but I'm sure there will be. Just think positive." Cindy got up and moved to the edge of the bed.

"But. . .but. . ." Beleaguered, Sarah's eyes teared up.

"Sarah. . .just rest now."

"How can I rest when my daughter is missing?"

"Listen to me. There are search teams out looking for her. I'm sure they're out there already. They have all kinds of ways to locate kids now. Be patient. You know it's all in God's hands. I called the camp office just after you left and spoke to the director there. They're on top of things. Are you with me?" Sarah nodded. "They know what they're doing. They've issued an Amber Alert bulletin and everything, and I saw it myself—the bulletin—it was on TV at the café on channel 6. They didn't waste any time, thankfully."

"I just wish I could be there to help. I feel so helpless." Sarah reached for a tissue on her tray table.

"Seriously Sarah? You've been hit by a truck. What did the doctor say?"

"He says I might need some kind of surgery."

Cindy frowned.

"Yeah, they're not sure yet, but I hope they figure it out soon."

"I hope so, too, but for now, you're in no shape to do anything. Best thing right now is to help yourself get better."

"I know, but I hate this. . .I can't stand it. . .not being there for her." A fresh wave of panic washed over her. "Thanks for coming up here, Cindy. You didn't need to do that."

"Oh, yes, I absolutely had to do that. Thank God I was on your emergency contact list. Besides, they canceled the camp. Everyone's rattled about it. Taylor is a mess."

Sarah's eyes brimmed in tears. "Oh, Cindy. . ."

"Don't worry, honey, it's only a matter of time before they find her."

Sarah wiped her eyes with the tissue and then pressed her good hand against her forehead.

"What's wrong?"

Sarah slowly shook her head. "Besides everything?"

"Is it your head. . .you alright?" Cindy got up and stepped toward the door. "I'm getting the nurse."

"No, no, Cindy, I'm fine. . .just tired. I'll be okay. Please don't bother the nurse. I've got a call button if I need her."

Cindy stopped at the doorway and turned around. "You sure, Sarah?"

She nodded.

"Well, if you're positive—"

"I am. I'll be okay."

Cindy sighed. "Okay, then I'm going to let you get some rest." At the doorway she waved. "I'll be back. Love you, girl."

Chapter Twenty-four

CRUISING THROUGH THE STREETS of downtown Bethlehem, Nick and Officer Jamison canvassed every street searching for Emily and Hayley or anyone who may have seen them walking in the neighborhood. They plastered storefronts and telephone poles with posters of the girls' headshots. NCIC was notified, along with other police districts who joined in from the surrounding counties.

"Two-forty," Officer Jamison said over the two-way radio. "Come in."

"Yeah, Earl, we've got a bunch of calls coming in. . .say they saw two girls fitting the description of the missing camp girls up at the Stacks last night."

"Copy, thanks." He hung up and turned to Nick. "We'll head there next."

Officer Jamison made a U-turn and traveled back via 3rd Street across town. "Think it's time to interview some folks up there. . .see what's doing."

A throng of people spread out over the panoply of outdoor cafés and shops in the entertainment district. Nick's energy ran high as he took in the crowd—all pleasantly chatting among themselves; their lives seemed intact. . .all wrapped up in their happy worlds and without a care. *She could be anywhere.* His eyes swept across the courtyard where children's laughter caught up in the breeze that carried a mix of scents permeating the air: suntan lotion, musk cologne, and rotisserie-grilled hotdogs. In the midst of the revelry, his mind kept reverting to images of Sarah—her hair grazing her cheek, and her piercing eyes peering straight into his heart. He longed to be with her even now. Despite the devastating situation with Emily's disappearance, the thought of Sarah pressed in on him. Her smile. Her voice. Her body. He could think of little else.

As his gaze roamed over the crowd, his heart skipped at the sight of two young girls. They stood staring into a storefront window, each holding a cup of water ice. The dark-haired girl resembled Emily to a T. His pulse picked up a beat. "Emily!" he called and stepped closer. "Emily?" Just as he was about to tap her on the shoulder, the other girl called out, "Hey, Christy." The girl in question turned her head, and he saw her resemblance fade. . .as did his hopes.

Chapter Twenty-five

LAZILY CANOEING ON THE Schuylkill River, Connor Stokes put down his fishing pole on the side of the canoe and cocked his head.

"Given up already, man?" his brother, Josh, said. "The day's barely started, dude."

"No, no. . .shhh." Connor shifted position and steadied his oars. "Back there"—he pointed—"did you hear that?"

The calm waters gently stirred underneath their canoe as the boat rocked gently. In the near distance, the sound of a faint cry carried across the rippling water.

"That!" Connor said. "Hear it?"

"Yeah."

"Sounds like a person, maybe? Or a sick cat." He adjusted the lens of the binoculars hanging from his neck as he panned the scene from one bank to the other.

"See anything?"

"Not really."

"Maybe it was just a squawking bird or something."

"Maybe, but. . ."

Their canoe drifted slowly down the river as the current carried it.

"I'm not seeing anything," Josh said after a while. "So, what do we do?"

Connor let go of the binoculars and grabbed an oar.

"Did you find something?"

"Don't know for sure. Let's turn around."

Josh threw down his pole. "Might as well. . .these fish aren't biting anyway."

In the quiet of early morning, Connor and his brother paddled their canoe down river, keeping a sharp eye on the outer banks for whatever made the odd sound.

"Spot the right side," Connor instructed. "I'll take the left."

As the canoe drifted, the sound came again. Connor slowed down his scanning and double backed. He saw something.

"There," he called to Josh. "See that?"

Josh squinted into the sunlight. "Something. . .looks like a white—"

"I think it's a person," Connor interrupted. "At the edge of the bank. Someone's definitely there." He grabbed his oars. "C'mon, let's go check it out." As the canoe drifted closer to the bank, Connor called out, "Hello, there!"

****

Emily lay shivering on the muddy bank as sunlight bounced off the water. Hearing the voices so close to her, she tried to raise her head again, curious as to who was calling. Were they calling to her? Was this a rescue or only a dream? She caught a glimpse as a jolt of pain ran up her spine, forcing her back down quickly.

Connor and Josh paddled up to the rocky bank and then got out of the boat and waded up to where Emily lay.

"Hey," Connor called out to her as he approached. "You alright?"

"My head. . .I hit my head." Her voice croaked.

Connor bent down beside her and examined the back of her head heavily crusted over with blood that coated the back of her neck and T-shirt.

"Okay. . .doesn't look good. We need to get you out of here." He gave her a sympathetic smile. "By the way, I'm Connor and this is Josh. What's your name?"

"Emily."

"How did you get here?"

Her body tensed at the reminder of the stalker—his raspy smoker's voice. She flinched at the memory. "I—well, me and my friend—we were trying to get back to our camp. . .and, well, this man had been following us. He was walking closer and closer and then. . .I just got scared and ran from him as fast as I could."

"Last night?" Connor asked.

"Uh huh. . .we were at the Stacks."

"What happened to your friend?"

Emily shrugged. "I wish I knew." Thoughts of the last time she'd seen Hayley came hazily to her mind.

Connor crouched down next to her. "Can you stand at all to make it out to the canoe?" He gestured toward it. "It's right over there."

Emily attempted to sit up. As her right hand brushed against her jeans, her face fell. "Wait. Oh, no!" she cried, patting her front pocket. "My cell phone. . ." Her stomach cinched. "It's gone."

"You had a phone?" Josh asked.

"Uh huh, but I must have dropped it. Oh, no. . .where is it?"

"When was the last time you had it?"

"Um, I really don't remember." Her eyes scanned over the rocks in the water. Panic set in. Did her phone somehow dislodge from her pocket and make its way into the river? She racked her brain thinking of when she last held it in her hand. "No, wait. I remember now. I think it's up there." She pointed behind her. "I'm pretty sure I left it up there between two rocks. Over there, I think. Not far. . .somewhere by that first boulder."

Josh turned and climbed up the side of the embankment along the larger boulders where she indicated. Meanwhile, Connor offered his hand. "Okay, let's try to sit up." He attempted to guide her to the canoe, but Emily's head spun as she started to push herself up out of the mud. "Ohhh," she groaned. "My head." She sat back down and held her head in her hands. "I feel dizzy."

"Uh oh." Connor frowned. "Okay, better remain still. Lie back down. We'll just lift you out to the canoe."

Moments later, Josh came back with a satisfied look on his face. "Is this what you're looking for?" He held up the phone.

Emily beamed as she took hold of her cell as though it were pure gold. "Oh my gosh, thank you so much!"

"So, you ready to go for a little ride?" Connor asked.

Emily nodded. Though inside she wasn't sure.

While the young men, each on either side, lifted Emily up, a wave of relief passed through her. She was headed for safety. Last night's bad dream was over. Josh and Connor together managed to carry Emily while sloshing their way out to the river. They carefully lowered her into the canoe and then hopped in themselves. Midway in buckling up his life jacket, Connor quickly undid the straps and handed the jacket to Emily. "Here, you'll need this," he said, and placed it over her head. "Buckle the straps here, okay?"

Grabbing their oars, the young men set off down the river in an effort to get Emily back to safety. The authorities would be able to handle things from there.

The river sparkled in the early morning sun. A few minutes later, Connor looked back at Emily as he and Josh rowed down river. "You doing okay?"

She nodded. "Uh huh."

"Sure?"

"Uh huh," she repeated, giving him a weak smile.

Connor gave her a thumbs up. "Great. . .hang in there."

As the canoe sailed downriver, a warm breeze blew across her face. The azure blue sky contrasted the green topped trees like crayon colors in her childhood coloring book. Although she felt safe with the two men, her thoughts buzzed about her head. *Are they worried for me back at the camp? Am I in trouble?* With all that happened to her over the past twelve hours, this adventure was like nothing she experienced before—not even in her worst nightmare. She'd never been out past bedtime before except for having to babysit for the neighbor down the hall. She mentally relived the nightmare of her ordeal while floating down the river with two strangers. What would her mother say to all of this? She must be worried sick.

"Water seems a bit choppy this morning." Connor looked back from where they'd come and saw the whitecaps in their wake. Josh frowned. "I know. . .and it's taking us faster, too."

Chapter Twenty-six

"Is that what I think it is?" Sam Stout stood overlooking the Schuylkill River while wrapping up his reel.

"What is?" his son, John, asked.

"That canoe."

"What about it?"

"It's getting awfully close to the barrier, son. Can you see that?"

"Uh-oh. Yeah, I see it now."

Sam quickly pulled out his cell phone. "Hey, this is Sam Stout calling from Pawlings Lock, Bethlehem Twp. Listen, there's a canoe heading toward the falls. Yep, less than a half-mile. Have no idea. . .nope, not right now. . .just lent it out. Okay, sure thing. Got it." The older man turned to his son. "River rescue is down on Black Rock right now. Said they've got an anchor."

"They're gonna need something," John said.

Both father and son jumped onto the cement boat launch and waved their hands wildly.

"Turn around!" they yelled. "Hey, turn the canoe around!" The oarsmen at the helm didn't seem to notice. The tiny canoe was headed for the falls. "They better see those markers soon," Sam said under his breath.

Sam's blood pressure rose as he remembered the *boil*—the turbulent recirculating stream that lurked directly out of sight, deep down under the surface. It is the most dangerous force in a low-head dam. The water flowing over the dam's face creates washing-machine-like turbulence that swallows everything and everyone in its course. The tumultuous rolling of the water formed a strong hydraulic force, dragging sailing vessels along the stream bed, then releasing them up to the surface of the water, then sucking them back into the face of the dam. This circulation can keep people, boats, and other objects trapped for an extended amount of time; the forces are brutal and largely inescapable. No matter how hard the struggle, the relentless hydraulic force that draws boaters will always come out stronger as it inevitably drags and batters the sailing vessel mercilessly against the dam's wall. While this was a serious situation for Sam's son, the young boy survived miraculously one of the most common and lethal hazards of low-head dams. His thoughts turned to what happened to his youngest son the day he'd been fishing a decade ago. Sam's knowledge of prevention and safety on the river became a priority after his son nearly died out on the water—a memory that haunted him ever since that day.

Although it wasn't his own flesh and blood out on the river in the canoe, all the same, Sam Stout's heart raced. He kept his eyes peeled on the canoe. Unfortunately, the surface of the water didn't pose a visible problem. No high rippling or anything unusual. No wonder they didn't notice the danger. *Inexperienced kids.* Everything seemed calm and peaceful as the water camouflaged the submerged hazard below. Another three hundred feet and they'd be goners. Impossible to make it out alive. The deadly picture pooled in his mind. . .now, he was re-living the nightmare all over again. His heart went out to the canoe sailing blissfully along in the otherwise picture-perfect river. *God, please help these folks. . .*

Chapter Twenty-seven

SARAH'S HEART BROKE AGAIN at the news the doctor announced. "I'm sorry, but it doesn't look good according to the tests. It's worse than we originally thought. Looks like your splenic artery is damaged and needs to be repaired. I'd recommend surgery," Dr. Byron, warned. "As soon as possible," he emphasized. His face knit with strong concern layered with sympathy.

Sarah's head spun. All this to deal with and her daughter missing, too. *God, how much more can I take?* As much as she felt like crying again, she forced herself to put on a brave face. "Whatever you say, doctor," she said with a sigh. "Do what you must."

"Sarah, I know what you're going through. It's daunting to say the least to not know where your daughter is. There's nothing I can do about that part of your life except help you to get better." He lent a professional smile. "And I'll be sure to do just that."

****

Cindy Holden sat in the waiting room of Lehigh Valley Hospital. She bought a Sudoku puzzle book from the gift shop to keep her mind occupied. She hated waiting, let alone compounding the wait with worry while her oldest and dearest friend was under the knife. It may as well have been her own sister on the operating table. Cindy tried to focus on the task at hand and worked on one of the puzzles. After completing one of the easier ones, she moved onto another on the next level and currently found herself stumped. She loved the challenge and hoped the extra concentration would keep her mind focused, but this time, her concern over Sarah trumped all. She glanced up at the clock for the hundredth time, wishing to stop the compulsion to monitor each minute. The clock seemed fueled by molasses.

As the time approached 2 p.m., there still was no notification that the operation was over. She looked up at the digital information panel. The bright red lights indicated each operation and the status—"in session," "post-op," or "in recovery." Sarah's status hadn't changed in over two hours. She got up and addressed the attendant.

"Excuse me, is the operation status accurate?" She pointed above to the digital sign. "I was hoping my friend was out of surgery by now."

"Yes, it should be accurate. Of course, there might be a short lag time, but. . ."

"Okay, I see," she replied with a nod and went back to the chair by the window. With an audible sigh, she picked up the puzzle book and tried to engage herself once more.

After another half-hour elapsed, Cindy's worry escalated. Sarah should have been out of the operation by now. Cindy knew a bit about laparoscopic surgery and all of the different scenarios of the surgery's protocols. As she understood things, Sarah's spleen only needed a repair. Didn't seem like too taxing job for the surgeon. *Was something wrong?*

****

Dr. Byron and his surgical team stood over the brightly lit operating table. He held onto the scalpel after making an upper midline incision just above the abdomen, deciding which direction to go. His mind spun with possibilities. With her abdominal cavity exposed, he surveyed the situation, perplexed at which direction to turn. He could either repair her spleen or take it out completely.

"Okay, we'll go laparoscopic," Dr. Byron announced.

"You sure?" the lead nurse asked.

"Yes, it's the best route. Judging from what I see here. . .less invasive."

"Her MRI shows the spleen to be rather large, but—"

"We're going laparoscopic," he replied, firmly.

"Okay, you're the doctor," she replied, respectfully.

The surgeon prepped and took his place at the table. He soon inserted the video camera tube into Sarah's abdomen and checked the monitor before proceeding. Minutes later, everything was going according to plan until something unusual happened.

"I'm seeing more blood than usual, doctor," the lead nurse said.

"So am I," he replied, sternly. "I don't like this." Dr. Byron took a double take at the monitor and then the abdominal cavity. "Is that a blood vessel tear?'

"Can't tell for sure. . .either severed or just torn," she said, adjusting her glasses.

Silence fell over the room. Under the heat of the overhanging light, the only sound was the heart monitor and Dr. Byron's sighs and curses.

"Damn! We may have to switch surgeries," he said, exasperated.

"To an open one?" the nurse asked.

"Yes, of course. What other is there?" he barked. "I didn't want to go there but seems like our only choice. She'll bleed out otherwise. Okay, let's regroup here—quick."

Partially into the procedure, changing horses in mid-stream was unsettling, at best, especially to Dr. Byron. With every minute counting, this interruption was a major distraction.

While the surgical team re-assembled, the surgeon went over the new instructions with the staff. Beginning once more, he made another incision into Sarah's abdomen and began the new procedure. Not long afterward, he shook his head as beads of sweat poured through his mask. Alarm spread over the team when the surgeon announced, "Damn, she's losing blood again."

"Losing blood," the lead nurse repeated while trying to remain calm.

"She needs blood!" the surgeon shouted. "Type and cross match ten units—start with two immediately."

"She's not stable," the technician announced. "Losing blood pressure. . .heartbeat is irregular."

"On it," Chief perfusionist Paul Louden replied as he set up the cell-saver machine.

"Doesn't look good," the technician yelled. "Hurry with the blood already or she'll code."

"Increasing her fluids now," the assistant nurse shouted while two others worked quickly to set up for the new blood.

Feverishly, the surgeon stared down into Sarah's abdomen. Blood gushed into the region. . .exactly what he tried to avoid by converting the procedure from what began as laparoscopic. Seconds ticked by as the surgery spiraled out of control and she was hemorrhaging more and more blood. Panicked, he realized his error. The hemodynamic situation resulted in an unstable condition for Sarah. Her life was now on the line. *Dear God, don't let her code.*

"He should have discontinued the surgery," the lead nurse whispered to the second nurse, who shrugged. "I tried to tell him."

"These surgeons think they're God or something," the other nurse whispered.

"Got that right." The lead nurse turned to the surgeon. "Repair or ligate?"

"Repair. . .it's only nicked."

As the new blood entered Sarah's body, Dr. Byron grabbed the sutures and both ends of the severed vein to suture it back together where the blood had been gushing. The operating team collectively held their breath as Dr. Byron performed the repair. Tensely, he worked under the hot lights as sweat drops dotted his forehead. Minutes later, he stood up, threw the sutures on the side table, and reached for a sterile towel.

"That should do it," he announced, wiping himself down.

The attendants all sighed with relief and smiles spread over everyone.

"She's a lucky woman," the technician said. "Good work, Dr. B."

At 4:00 p.m., Sarah was admitted to the ICU. Outside in the waiting room, Cindy glanced up again at the information panel.

"Finally!" she exclaimed.

The receptionist lent a hint of a smile.

"It reads that she's in ICU now. Is that standard procedure?"

"Sometimes," the receptionist replied. "It's sometimes a holding station for precautionary reasons until they can find her a room."

"Oh, okay." The knot in Cindy's stomach began to loosen a bit. At least, the operation was over.

Chapter Twenty-eight

"You're doing great, Emily." Connor gave her the thumbs up sign again as they canoed down the river. "We're almost where we need to be, honey."

"Hey," Josh said. "Those two guys. . .Connor, do you see them?"

"Where?"

"On that cement thing."

"The boat launch?"

"Looks like they're calling out to us."

Connor panned his gaze up and down the river. "Well, guess so, we're the only ones on the river."

"What?" Josh called out over the water. "Can't hear them. . .say, what?" he repeated.

"Hold up, Josh," Connor commanded his brother. He stopped rowing and turned a keen ear.

As Sam and John yelled out for them to turn around, they both pointed ahead toward the dam.

"Looks like they're pointing to something, Connor."

Connor froze. *The buoy markers.* They must have missed them. In his quest to bring Emily to safety, his only concern was for the girl. He hadn't even noticed what he knew better to avoid.

"Oh, great. I'm an idiot," Connor yelled. "They're warning us to turn around. The dam ahead—it's not good, Josh. . .we're getting too close. *Oh, Lord, please.* The canoe was drifting at a good pace even without the rowing. "Quick, turn this thing around," he yelled.

Josh did as he was told, and together they shifted direction. They paddled as fast as they could to avoid drifting. At one point, Josh had so much momentum going, he accidentally thrust too hard and lost his grip on the oar.

"Damn," he shouted.

"Yes, the damn—it's almost on top of us! How could I be so-so stupid. Keep paddling. Just paddle."

"No, the oar, Connor. I lost my *oar*!"

"What? Oh, man. . .for Pete's sake. How'd you do that?"

"I don't know, but I did is all. . .just slipped." He moved to the back of the boat and began to undress.

"No, Josh. It's too late. Don't even think about going in for it," warned Connor. "It's too far back, and there's no time." Connor pulled one of his oars out of the water. "Here, take one of mine."

Meanwhile, Connor paddled the canoe furiously in the opposite direction of the buoy markers. Frantic now that all three lives were at stake, his adrenaline flooded at warp speed as he fought the current that slowly pulled them toward the point of no return.

****

The rescue boat sped across the river. "We're almost there," said Ron Daniels, Bethlehem Township River Rescue unit leader.

"Yep, I've spotted them. . .a canoe with three on board," partner Jim Fried said.

Binoculars in hand, Ron spotted them, too. "Got 'em in sight. . .they're mighty close to danger. This could be a challenge."

"Yep, as long as we don't get too close."

"Got that right. They don't call it the *Death Machine* for nothing. Hopefully, we won't lose another to that menace." Ron gunned the engine faster. "Got the anchor ready?"

"Right here."

"Ropes secured?"

"Got 'em."

"Okay, let's roll in. We don't have much time here."

"Connor!" Josh called out. "Look!"

Connor turned to see a boat storming up the river.

"It's help on the way," Josh cried. "Thank God!"

Connor sighed with relief. *Thank God is right.*

Both of them waved their hands signaling their distress as the rescue boat approached.

"Hey!" Ron yelled through a megaphone. "Rescue here. . .I need you to listen up."

Connor's heart pounded as he fought to focus on what the man was saying while panicking that the buoy markers to the low head damn were inching closer by the minute.

"Are we going to. . .oh, I'm scared," Emily cried.

"It's okay, honey. We'll be fine," he said as calmly as he could. There was no way he could move from his position to wrap his arm around her or comfort her as he would have liked. Josh would have to do that. "Just hang tight."

In a matter of minutes, Connor watched as the rescuers took an anchor and threw it as close to the canoe as they could. He struggled to reach for the rope attached to it with the help of Josh, who pulled the rope behind him. Once the anchor was secured, the rescue boat slowly pulled them back to safety.

Chapter Twenty-nine

SARAH OPENED HER EYES. Her lips curled in an attempted smile.

"Hey, how're ya doing, there?" Cindy whispered.

"Guess I made it okay, huh?"

"Yes, you did, sweetie. . .you're out of surgery."

"Fixed my spleen, did they?"

Cindy nodded. "You'll be fine. . .just rest for now. I just wanted you to know I'm here. Joe wanted to come, but he got called in to work. Sends his love."

Sarah, sleepy-eyed, nodded. "Tell him I say—oh, ah. . .damn."

"You okay?"

Sarah shook her head and squeezed her eyes as she grimaced. "Ow, it hurts bad."

"Your stomach? Head? Where, Sarah?"

"My side," she said, pointing to her incision. "Oww."

"I better get the nurse for you." Cindy darted from the room into the hall.

"Miss Sarah," the nurse announced as she hustled into the room, followed by Cindy, who lingered behind. "Heard you're in a little bit of pain, dear."

Sarah barely nodded.

"It's to be expected. . .don't be alarmed." She adjusted the IV fluids and checked all of the connections. "We'll just give you a bit more pain meds to help you, okay?"

Sarah mouthed *thank you.*

The nurse paused for a moment and, seeming confident with the situation, turned and slipped out the door.

As the pain in Sarah's side slowly eased, she closed her eyes and drifted to sleep. Cindy said a quick prayer for her friend.

"I'll be back, Sarah," she whispered and left the room.

****

"You guys are pretty lucky," Lead rescuer Ron Daniels perched his hands on his hips.

Connor just shook his head in mock disdain. "Yep. Thanks to you guys."

"Yeah, thanks," Josh repeated.

"That low-rise dam is a killer should you get caught in it. . .like a deadly washing machine." Ron cocked his head toward the river.

"I know. I'm so stupid to miss those markers." Connor shook his head again. "I took my contacts out because they were bothering me and. . .well. . .all I can say is thank you."

"Well, that's what we're here for."

"How'r you doing, sweetheart?" Ron asked Emily.

"Better now," she replied.

"Um, by the way," Connor began. "This is Emily. We found her on the bank earlier this morning. The police need to be notified."

"Already on it," Ron said. "Heard the alert on the radio. We placed the call."

"Should be here soon," Jim announced. "Yep, think that's them now."

Ron crossed his arms over his burly chest and questioned Connor and Josh. "You sure about that?"

"What are you saying?" Connor asked.

"I'm asking if you're sure is all." His eyes pierced through like black stones.

Connor raised his hands in mock surrender. "What? You think we kidnapped her or something?"

"There's a bulletin out for her."

"Seriously?" Connor barked. "Well,"—he glanced at his brother—"we didn't know anything about it. We were fishing when we spotted her."

Ron's eyes bore into him. "Not saying I think it, but. . ."

Connor turned to Emily. "Emily, could you please tell the man how we found you this morning. . .you know, what happened to you?"

Emily sat with her knees tucked under her chin. She just smiled and said, "They rescued me, sir. I was out in the woods alone all night."

Ron dropped his arms. "Well, for Pete's sake. Pardon me for being so suspicious, but you. . .well, you know it's a crazy world. Weirder things have happened."

Just then, the police pulled up in the parking lot adjacent to the boat launch followed by an ambulance. Nick and Officer Jamison exited the car.

"Morning, gentlemen," Ron called over to them as they made their way toward the river bank.

Officer Jamison nodded as Nick rushed toward them. "Heard you found her. . .Emily Harding?"

Ron beamed. "Yes, sir. We got her. She's right over there." He pointed a stubby finger in her direction. "Doesn't seem to be in too bad a shape, but the two young gentlemen over there, they found her first. This morning, in fact. Apparently, she hit her head, they said. Should be checked out for sure."

"We'll run her right over to the hospital," Officer Jamison said, looking over to the ambulance while Nick hustled past them toward the river where Emily sat. "Good work, fellas." He saluted Connor and Josh. Officer Jamison checked out the boat in the river and asked, "Is that the new Rescue Craft I've been hearing about?"

"Yep, sure is. . .ResQDek. . .it's the latest thing out there. We can get right into the boiler current—that is, if we have to, God forbid. Only this time, we just had to use the anchor."

"So, what all happened?"

"They got too close to the low-rise dam."

"The canoe?"

"Yep, caught 'em just in time before they got pulled into the hydraulic undertow."

"Nice work."

"Emily!" Nick shouted as he approached the riverbank.

Emily perked up and turned her head. "Nick!" Tears came to her eyes as he ran toward her.

He smiled broadly as they embraced. "Em, we were so worried. Are you okay?"

She nodded as she sobbed. "I'm okay."

He gently wiped her tears away with his finger.

"You sure, honey?"

"I guess. . .well, except for my head." She raised her hand to feel the lump.

Nick frowned. "What happened to your head?"

"I must've gotten knocked out when I fell on the rocks."

He reached for the back of her head. "Yeah, you've got a goose egg there for sure. But we'll get you all checked out soon. But I need to ask you. . .what happened? What happened to you and your friend? Why were you out here?"

"Oh, Nick, it was awful. I was sooo scared," she explained as they walked toward the ambulance. "Just awful. Me and Hayley were at this place, a really cool place, and then we were walking back and then this—"

"Okay, young lady," Officer Jamison interrupted. "These gentlemen are going to take you to the hospital. We need to get you checked out."

"Can Nick come with me?"

"Absolutely."

"What hospital?" Nick asked.

"Lehigh Valley."

Chapter Thirty

IN THE DESCENDING ELEVATOR, Cindy prayed for Sarah. What could she do besides pray? Of course, prayer was the most important thing at times like these, and Cindy's faith remained strong. She hoped Sarah hadn't lost hers. Cindy mused on the impact of all that happened to Sarah in the past seven hours. Picturing her own daughter, Taylor, in the same position as Emily, brought her grief to another level. What if the roles were reversed? *But for the grace of God. . .*

The elevator pinged. At the lobby, Cindy stepped off and spotted the sign posted on the wall designating locations and directions. At seeing the arrow for the gift shop, she immediately knew what do. *Yes, flowers.* They would be good to help bring some cheer and, hopefully, hasten the healing process. Besides praying, what else could a friend do at this time? Her heart grieved for the woman. Between Sarah's body having taken a beating as well as her torn heart for her beloved missing daughter, the stress was over the top. Prayers, flowers, visits. . .it was all she could do to help. Cindy hoped there was something better on the horizon for her dearest friend.

The warm aroma of browning meat emanated from the cafeteria farther down the hall. The scent beckoned her and her stomach growled. She'd purchase the flowers later. Right now, as she hadn't eaten all day, she needed something.

Inside the cafeteria, Cindy picked up a tray and headed for the hot bar. Everything looked good to a starving stomach, but hot slices of meatloaf drenched in brown gravy called the loudest. She ordered some with a side of steamed broccoli and brown rice. Not bad for hospital food. After paying she took a seat by the window and watched as people came into and out of the hospital.

The view from where she sat opened onto the "A" parking lot in front of the hospital where the main driveway connected to the highway through town. As visitors approached the front entrance, she studied their demeanor and wondered whether theirs would be a happy visit to welcome a daughter's new baby, or one where someone they knew and loved was going through a tough time or cancer treatments?

Cindy finished her meal and placed her tray on top of the waste disposal bin before heading back out to the hallway in search of the gift shop. Once inside, the offerings were slim, but she wouldn't leave without purchasing something. After she waded through the aisles of trinkets, gadgets, toys, along with a collection of stuffed animals and other knickknacks, she noticed a tiny refrigerated unit. Inside were the flowers she'd hoped to find—sprays of roses, baby's breath, carnations and lacelike ferns all arranged in milk glass vases. *Perfect.*

****

The ambulance made its way toward the hospital. Emily laid on the gurney with Nick by her side while the EMT took her vitals. "Patient checks out fine. . .heart and BP normal," he announced. "All except that gash to your head," he said with a reserved smile. "But they'll get you all fixed up, don't worry."

"Almost there, Em," Nick consoled while holding her hand. "Another minute and we'll be there. . .just beyond the next traffic light. Hang in there."

"I've never been in an ambulance before," she said to him. Wide-eyed, she glanced all around.

"Let's hope you never do again."

Cindy went back to Sarah's room with the bouquet of flowers in hand. At the approach to her room, she paused at the threshold. Sarah's eyes were still closed. Moving quietly to the bedside, Cindy heard the steady breathing of a sound sleep. Happy for Sarah that she was getting some much needed rest and seeing it was a peaceful sleep not fraught with tossing and turning, she quietly placed the vase of flowers on the tray table where Sarah would be able to see them the moment she awoke. Cindy knew mere flowers wouldn't erase the pain in her friend's heart for all that she was going through, both physically and emotionally, but hopefully it would lend a glimpse of beauty that could lighten the load, if only for the moment.

Cindy moved over to the window to place a quick call to her husband to check in. "Hey, hon, it's me." While on the call, something familiar drew and held her eye. Outside, standing at the back of the ambulance parked in the emergency entrance three stories below appeared to be a guy who resembled Nick Durham. *Hmmm. . .? Was that really him or his double?*

"Joey, gotta go now." Puzzled, she peered out the window. "Yeah, I'll be home as soon as I can. Probably after dinner though. Mind making dinner for yourself? Okay. . .thanks. Yeah, I'll be fine. I'll get dinner at the café here. The food isn't bad. Okay, talk to you later." She hung up and saw Sarah still in a deep sleep. That was fine with her because she had more pressing things to do.

Cindy made haste down to the lobby. Passing through the double doors, she hastened for the Emergency room. In the near distance, the ambulance she'd just seen remained parked. Her heart jolted at the sound and sight of ambulances, never knowing whether the person on board was near death or not, and she was always in the habit of offering up a quick prayer for those on board. This time was no exception. As she approached, there was no gurney visible nor anyone else around. She went back inside through the emergency entrance. She looked all around for the guy she saw only minutes ago. There was only one Nick Durham. Tall, dark hair, piercing light eyes. . .and dreamy. Sarah was lucky to have had him in her life. Too bad their relationship hit a snag, she mused.

Amid the scene of the controlled chaos, Cindy glanced around the area, hoping to catch a glimpse of the Nick Durham look-alike. Unfortunately, the waiting room held at least a dozen people, but there was no one resembling him. Her heart ached for the ill folks who needed help and were forced to wait. An emergency room shouldn't have to be so crowded, yet they usually were. Horror stories of people with sickness and illnesses having to wait four, five, six or more hours flashed in her head. She'd read about them on Facebook and knew of others from friends and family members. And here they were—young and old—all waiting, desperate for medical attention.

Cindy stood by the emergency check-in station and watched as hospital personnel hustled in and out of the double doors leading to the emergency room. As the doors opened, she caught a glimpse of a figure standing down the hall by a curtained room. Her heart lightened. *Is that Nick? Could it be him?* Just then the TV monitor in the waiting room caught her attention as the Breaking News graphic appeared. Cindy looked up as the picture of a girl flashed on the screen. Her eyes glued to the image on the TV. Her breath caught and her heartbeat kicked up a notch. The anchor's voice held an optimistic tone as she announced that Emily Harding had been found alive and was safe. *Oh, thank God!*

Chapter Thirty-one

OVER JOYED WITH THE news about Emily, Cindy bubbled with excitement and didn't know what to do. Tell Sarah? Go find the look-alike? In a quandary, trapped in an emotional stalemate, her eye caught sight of the double doors opening once more. She moved closer and peered down the hall before they closed again. As much as she wanted to run up to Sarah's room, she would do that, sure, but right now her curiosity grew even more when, finally, she spotted the man again.

"Nick? she called out from the entry way. Not knowing whether she was allowed to enter, she took a bold step inside and paused as the door closed behind her. Nervously, she stood still for a moment. No alarm went off. She relaxed knowing everything was cool. There was no one else around. All of the movement and action seemed to be contained at the farthest end of the long hallway. She kept her eye pinned to the look-alike and called out his name again after taking tentative steps down the hallway. The man turned his head.

"Nick!"

"Cindy?"

"Oh, Nick. They found her!"

"Yes, I know." He pointed to the curtain drawn across the front of one of the emergency cubicles. "The doctor's is checking her out right now."

Cindy couldn't wipe the smile off of her face. "Oh, this is too wonderful." She reached out and flung her arms around him. "So, you were there when they found her? Where was she? Is she okay?"

Nick nodded. "She's fine. I was with the police. We got the call and then went to the river—the Schuylkill River. That's where they found her up near the old Bethlehem Steel property. Apparently, some kids found her—two boys in a canoe. She hit her head when she fell on the river bank. . .got knocked out, but other than that. . ." He shrugged. "Happy ending. . .but what are you doing here? How did you know Emily would be brought here?"

Cindy stepped away as Nick was speaking and peaked inside the curtain to see Emily lying on the table while the doctor and an assistant spoke with her. Aside from looking a bit pale, she didn't look much different. She dropped the curtain and turned back to him. "I'm so glad everything turned out okay. What a relief. And what a relief it'll be for Sarah. . .but, oh, Nick. I have some not-so-good news." Nick's expression changed as though what light was inside him suddenly darkened. "I'm here because Sarah was in an accident."

"Is she alright?"

"Car accident. . .on the Northeast Extension."

"Is she alright?" he repeated, the anxious tone in his voice rose.

"Yes, yes, she's alive and all. Just some internal injuries. And she's here."

His eyes blinked quickly. "*Where* is she?"

"She's here, Nick."

"Here?"—he pointed to the floor—"As in *this* hospital?

Cindy nodded. "Yes. She's on the fourth floor, room 408.

Chapter Thirty-two

"THE GIRL LOOKS TO be okay from what we see," the doctor said regarding Emily. "Everything checks out—blood pressure, reflexes. . .of course, the bump on her head will take some time to heal, but there are no signs of permanent damage or trauma."

"No concussion?" Nick asked.

"No hydrocephalus or serious damage. . .just some contusions," the doctor explained. "We did a CT scan and gave her some mild pain relievers. Actually, she's a lucky girl."

Nick nodded affirmatively. "Great to hear."

"I'd keep an eye out on her sleeping patterns and wakefulness. . .also, her moods and that sort of thing."

"Um, actually, I'm not her guardian. . .just a friend of her mother." He turned to Cindy. "She's probably the one who should know."

"Yes, as I was saying," the doctor continued. "She may experience some negative changes. . .some mood swings, and she'll need to get as much rest as possible in the next few days."

"Such good news, doctor." Cindy smiled. "Her mother will be thrilled." She turned to Nick. "By the way has she been told yet about Emily?"

Nick shrugged. "You know, I don't really know—"

"Well, someone needs to tell her right away!" Cindy blurted out. She immediately darted down the hallway looking for someone to tell. She found someone in a lab coat and pulled her aside to explain the situation.

"We'll be sure to get the message to her right away," the lab assistant replied.

"Thank you!" Cindy said, holding her hands together on her chest. Cindy went back and peeked inside the curtain. "May we go in now?" she asked the doctor.

He extended his arm and gestured to go ahead.

"Hey, Em!" Cindy said upon entering the cubicle.

"Aunt Cindy!"

Cindy went to Emily's bedside and wrapped her arms around her. "You sure had us so worried about you."

"I'm okay."

"We were all praying for you, Em."

"I thought I was going to die out there."

"Well, you're safe now."

"I was so scared."

"I'm sure you were. . .the river is a scary place to be—especially, at night."

"Even before that, I was scared. When the man was asking us—"

"A man? What man?"

"Yeah, this man was talking to us—"

"Did he touch you?"

"No, no, but when Hayley and I were walking back to the dorm, this guy started walking toward us on the street. He didn't look cool at all. I mean, it made me feel so uncomfortable, like he was evil or something. I just got a bad feeling like in a movie when the scary music starts up. I knew this probably was a bad scene."

Cindy sucked in a breath and shook her head. "So, he never laid a hand on you, right?"

Emily nodded. "But then we got scared and ran—actually, I got scared and just felt I needed to run. I don't know where Hayley went, but I just ran as fast as I could away from him."

"Have you told the police all of this?" Cindy asked.

"They questioned her and she gave them her statement," Nick offered.

"That's good. I'm sure you were frightened, but it's all over now, Em. You're totally safe now."

"It was a nightmare."

"I'm sure it was, honey."

"I've been trying to reach my mom"—she held up her cell phone—"but there's no answer."

"Honey, about your mom." She folded her hands together and glanced over at Nick. "Well, listen," Cindy began, "your mom will be more than delighted to see you. In fact, she's right here in the hospital."

Emily brightened. "Here? Where is she?"

"Yes, Em." Cindy's voice softened. "Listen, I don't want you to worry or anything, but your mom had an accident—"

Emily's hand flew to her mouth. "A car accident. . .is she okay?"

"Yes, with the car. But she's okay. She is in good hands and will be better soon. May take a little while. For now, though, she just needs to rest."

"Can I see her?"

"I'm sure you can. You'll go up with us, right Nick?"

Nick lowered his head and seemed to shrink back at the idea. Not making eye contact with her, he mumbled something incoherent.

"Nick, you okay?"

He lifted his eyes to her. "Yeah, yeah, I'm fine."

"So, you'll come up, too?"

Nick hesitated. "Cindy, you know we broke up and everything. I don't really think it's my place to. . ."

"Nick? Are you serious?" She plopped both hands onto her hips. "Seriously, Nick. You came all the way up here to help find Emily, and now you want to bow out when the glory comes along? Doesn't make sense to me."

Nick's face turned sullen. "You *are* concerned, Nick, for Sarah. . .I can see it in your eyes." She led him outside of the curtain to speak more privately and not in front of Emily.

"Yes, of course, I am," he whispered. "I just don't feel as comfortable as I'd like is all. After all, she's the one who broke up with *me*, remember?"

"I thought you walked out on *her*?"

He dug his hands into his pockets and shook his head. "Sure, to save face. She'd already given me the boot. What else could I do? Not going to be a chump."

"Okay, so she broke up with you. Right now, her life is on the line, and Emily adores you. So, do the right thing. Come upstairs with us. I'm sure Sarah will be glad to see you—all of us, really."

Nick dug his hands deeper into his pockets. "Yeah, well, two out of three, maybe."

Cindy put her hand on his arm. "C'mon, Nick. Let's not go there."

Chapter Thirty-three

SARAH STIRRED WHILE THE nurse stood by her bedside.

"Miss Sarah, you have visitors here to see you."

Sarah opened her eyes and her lips spread into a broad smile.

"Mom!" cried Emily as she flew to her mother's side. "Mom, are you going to be okay? They said you were in an accident."

Sarah reached out with one arm as tears spilled from her eyes. Seeing her daughter gave her sensory overload. Her joy ballooned.

"Oh, Emily. . ."—her tears turned to sobs—"I'm so-so glad to see you, baby," she cried. "I was so worried. . .worried sick." She attempted to sit up while the nurse put another pillow behind her.

While mother and daughter held each other's hand, something caught Sarah's eye. She glanced up at the TV monitor in the corner of the room. Just then, images of both Emily and Hayley lit up the screen.

"Hey"—a huge grin spread over Sarah's face as she pointed to the TV—"Look!"

They all glanced up at the TV where the local newscast was doing another segment on the disappearance of the girls. The volume remained on mute, but the smile on the female anchor's face said it all.

"I'm famous!" cried Emily with delight.

From her bedside, Sarah took in the unbelievable moment that her daughter had been found safe and sound. The moment overwhelmed her.

"Yep, you sure are, honey," Sarah said.

"But where's Hayley?" Emily asked. "Did they find her, too?"

"Not sure, honey," Cindy said. "I wish I could tell you."

Sarah proceeded to pepper her daughter with questions, one after the other, about what had happened and all that went down that fateful night. Emily explained the details of the incident to her mother and aunt as best as she could. At one point, Emily stopped talking and glanced around the room.

"Hey, where's Nick?" Emily asked, turning her head toward the doorway. Nick stood just outside the threshold of Sarah's room; his hands were stuffed into his pockets. "Nick," she called and beckoned him in. "Mom, Nick was there to rescue me, too."

Sarah's eyes shot to the door. Though things felt a bit fuzzy in her head from a combination of restless sleep and the meds the doctors prescribed, Sarah saw Nick the way she'd always remembered him: shy, low-key, and always her hero. Nick slowly walked into the room.

"Nick," Sarah said, softly, as though he'd given her the moon.

"Hey, Sarah." His face remained stoic, though in his eyes she could see something sparkle.

Her mind spun with thoughts like a tumbling dryer. Thoughts of them together—the good times, the bad—all flashed around in the cycle of their season together. They hadn't been together for more than a year, but there were enough good times to muse over. The images weaved themselves in her mind, and though she couldn't quite come to a conclusion about how she felt—at least not exactly—her mood lightened and her pulse kicked up a notch. Having her daughter safely back was exceedingly above what she could ask God for. But seeing Nick there in the flesh and knowing that he had a part in finding Emily, made the moment all the sweeter. *Was it the meds or Nick himself giving her this wonderful high?*

Nick approached Sarah's bed. "So, how are you doing?"

Sarah never felt worse but didn't let on. The splenectomy had taken its toll and left her totally drained, and without any make-up on, she was embarrassed and self-conscious to be around anyone in the harsh, unforgiving fluorescent light of the hospital room, let alone Nick. Though seeing Nick for the first time in months, she felt more energized by the minute. Her self-consciousness lingered but something else rose up as well. *What's happening here?*

"I guess I'll survive." She lent a weak smile. "Good to see you."

"I'm sure you will, Sarah. . .sorry about the accident."

A long pause rose between them. He rested his hand on the bed rail and waited as though he had something more to say. Sarah could see he was searching for the words and had no clue what he wanted to say to her after all of these months apart. Yet she felt a stirring inside her. "Hey, thank you for helping find Emily. . .really sweet and brave of you, Nick."

Nick bowed his head slightly. Sarah could see a glimmer in his eye. "The cop in me had to get to the bottom of it."

Sarah smiled. *That was so Nick. . .always the hero.*

"She's a good kid."

Sarah nodded. "I know."

"The moment I heard—it was Cindy who told me—I felt a bolt of lightning tear through me." His lips curled into a sweet smile.

"You guys always did get along well."

Nick nodded while locking eyes with her. The power of the moment sent an electric surge through her whole body. Once again, the connection between them was palpable. The energy ran deep. Despite her bedridden state, an overwhelming sense of peace came over her. Her mood lightened, and something inside shifted. Her heart leaped like an untethered balloon about to lift up from out of her chest. Her eyes roamed over his face and lowered toward his body. His physique had always captured her attention. Standing there in his blue oxford shirt with the sleeves rolled up, her reaction to his masculinity took her by surprise. By now, she truly couldn't even remember what they broke up over.

Just then, the nurse came into the room, followed by Dr. Byron.

"Sorry to interrupt the party here," Dr. Byron said with a smile. "Just wanted to check in to see how you were feeling, Sarah.

Your most recent numbers show your RBC and WBC are still a bit off; so, we need to keep an eye on them, but I feel confident that we can release you in a day or so. How does that sound?"

Sarah smiled. "Sounds great, doctor. I'm all for going home. . .just a bit tired right now."

"That's to be expected. How's your pain threshold?"

"Pain is lessening," she replied.

The doctor nodded. "Scale of one to 10?"

Sarah paused. "About a five."

He nodded again. "Sounds about right for the size of the incision. Pain meds will help until things completely heal." The doctor made some notations on her chart and then put his hand on her shoulder. "You're making great progress," he said. "And I heard about your daughter"—he turned to Emily who sat by the window—"That right there will help you heal in no time." He lent a confident grin. "You should be on the mend very soon."

"Thank you, doctor," Sarah said as Cindy and Nick both looked on with smiles.

Chapter Thirty-four

Three months later

4:30 p.m.

"Over there, Em," Sarah said, pointing across the room. "Every box with the word *bedroom* I'll need you to take care of, okay?"

Sarah scanned the room. *Where to start?* A mound of boxes sat like an eyesore in the middle of the living room of her new condo. Things had finally come together for her, and Sarah couldn't be any happier than to have her own unit at Greenbrier Hills. Finally, her money would get the advantage of being stockpiled into an investment—one that could lend her security for a rainy day and not be poured down the proverbial rat hole. She put a hand on her hip and sighed. The hardest part of moving was getting things back where they belonged. Like standing on the deck of a ship in high tide without any mooring, she couldn't wait until she got her footing back and her life was settled once more.

Sarah opened one of the boxes marked *hallway*. At that moment, her mind reeled back to the old apartment and her life there. Memories from over the years flooded back. The faces of her closest neighbors-turned-friends ebbed and flowed in and out and kept her thinking about how they were doing, especially Winny. How she'd hated to leave the poor woman. So many good things to remember—the kindly doorman, Max, who'd been such a bright spot for so many of the residents who passed through the lobby every day . . . Mr. Kramer and his attentiveness over the years to whatever issues anyone dealt with. Of course, the charming location of the building that sat like a gem among a copse of lush, privacy-lending oak trees would always remain a distant treasure. A veil of sadness overcame her at reminiscing about her next-door neighbor, Beth Benson.

Sarah unpacked the items in the box and began to place them in the hallway closet. As she unpacked box after box, her thoughts focused on the day when she'd heard the news that had left her reeling. . .

Seven weeks earlier. . .

A knock at the apartment door startled Sarah one morning shortly after her release from the hospital. It surprised her that anyone would come calling at that hour. Still wearing her robe and feeling groggy, she shuffled out of the kitchen to get to the door. A look through the peephole revealed her neighbor, Beth Benson, standing in the hallway. Sarah opened the door. Beth's swollen, red eyes immediately gave her mood away.

"Beth. . .are you alright?"

Beth stood like a shaking tree. He pallor appeared white as porcelain, and her eyes glistened as she mopped up her tears with a crumpled tissue. She cupped her face with both hands. "Not good."

In sympathy, Sarah reached out to touch Beth's shoulder. "Beth, come in. What happened?" Sarah stepped back and beckoned her neighbor to the sofa. "Sit down. . .do you want some juice or coffee? I was just about to pour myself a cup."

Beth shook her head. "No, no, but thanks."

"Are you sure?"

The woman nodded quickly. "I'm fine, really."

"You don't look fine. Tell me what's going on."

Beth frowned. "It's not good—"

"Wait, hold on. Let me get my coffee first. Sorry, but I need the caffeine."

Beth nodded again. "I'll bet." Her voice came out thin and strained. "I was praying for you when I heard you were in the hospital."

"Thanks," Sarah called from the kitchen. "I needed all the prayers I could get. . .still do. I'm not completely out of the woods yet." She came back into the living room carrying two mugs of coffee and placed them on the table. Then she sat on the high back chair across from Beth. "So, tell me. What's going on?"

Beth twisted the ball of tissue in her hands. "It's my daughter."

Sarah recalled the awful incident when Emily and Hayley had disappeared from the hockey camp. While Emily had been found, Hayley remained missing after being kidnapped and nearly died in an accident on the roadway after jumping to make her escape out of a moving vehicle. The oncoming car swerved out of the way but clipped her as it careened down the embankment. Turned out the abductor was wanted on fraud charges in addition to the kidnapping of the teenage girl.

Sarah lost track of the case in the midst of her own health issues at the hospital, but she recalled snippets of the newscasts about the story. It ran for more than a week as new developments came forth. She'd been so overwhelmed with everything—including her own daughter's turbulent situation as well as the reemergence of Nick in her life. Facing health issues on top of everything, Sarah was overloaded mentally, physically, and emotionally.

"How is Hayley doing these days? Doing better now, I hope."

"She's still in the wheelchair. Probably will be for a while. . .maybe forever? Who knows."

"A wheelchair?" Beth's words knocked her out and Sarah dropped her head for a second. "Seriously? Oh, I'm so sorry to hear that."

Tears pooled in Beth's eyes. "Hopefully, her leg will mend normally, but the doctors haven't given us anything definite to bank on." She dabbed her eyes and then picked up the mug of coffee. "It just looks hopeless for now."

"Must be so difficult for her."

"For both of us. . ."

"I'm sure."

"I keep asking God what is the purpose for all of this?"

Sarah related to the question. "Tell me about it. . .God has his ways, that's for sure."

"Sometimes, it seems like it's *His* world and we just live in it."

Sarah nodded. "Got that right."

"Is she going to rehab or. . .?"

"Rehab is where she's staying now. It's an assisted living place in Pottstown."

"How's it going for her?"

Beth let out a sigh. "As well as can be expected. For Hayley, it's not a good place at all. She hates it but is making the best of it. I mean, what choice is there?"

Sarah's heart went out to Beth inwardly, but she had no clue how to comfort her bereaved neighbor. With Hayley now handicapped, there was nothing Sarah could say that would change the situation or make it better. Ameliorating a rotten situation with mere words seemed too superficial for Sarah to even attempt at this point. The only thing she could offer was her time, prayers, and support.

Silence rose in the room. Sarah sensed there was something else pressing on Beth's mind and heart. Beth stared down at the table and twisted the balled-up tissue with both hands.

"Is there anything else you need?" Sarah spared her own words, not wanting to be too pushy or demand that Beth open up to her, but Sarah got the impression Beth had something else on her mind and tried to encourage her to open up about it. "If you want to—"

"Sarah," Beth said, softly interrupting. "There' a bigger issue here that I need to share with you."

Sarah stiffened at seeing Beth's face go from grieving to serious. "Okay, sure. It's all good. You can share it with me."

Beth slowly shook her head. "No, it's not all good. Not even close." She paused. "You're not going to like it, Sarah. In fact, it's rather distressing for both of us."

Sarah cocked her head. "So, what is it?"

"It's something I found."

"Okay," Sarah said, shifting in her seat.

"Brace yourself," Beth began. "Frankly, I can't even believe it's true. Never in a million years would I have believed it."

Sarah waited patiently. It was obvious that Beth was not comfortable sharing what was on her mind and kept stalling for time. Fortunately, Sarah hadn't planned anything for the day, and her schedule remained light as far as chores and errands. Since leaving the hospital, Emily had, miraculously picked up the slack in helping out with the housework and doing things that Sarah normally would do. It was as though the girl suddenly grew up in just a few months since the episode on the river. The awful night had generated a new lease on life, and the girl took her cues and stepped up. So, it was obvious now that Sarah's sole purpose today was to be a listening ear to her neighbor.

"I'm listening." Sarah took one last sip of her coffee and put down the mug. She sat back and folded her hands in her lap, bracing for whatever it was that would shock her as Beth began to describe the details of what she found. . .

****

Beth paused to reflect back on the day when she encountered the unimaginable in her daughter's room. Hayley's bedroom couldn't have been more of a mess when Beth came in to gather her daughter's clothes strewn on the floor, obviously needing laundering. The unmade bed could have used a stripping down as well, so she pulled off the sheets and pillow cases and piled them into the laundry basket. While in her daughter's room, Beth lent a cursory glance and started to straighten up all that needed attention beginning with the crooked dresser mirror, table tops of loosely tossed magazines, assorted candles, and miscellaneous bottles of perfume, lotion, and nail polish. Beth hated seeing the clutter, and she took the time to arrange things more orderly, hoping that when Hayley returned home from hockey camp, her life might be a little more orderly as well. That was the main reason she'd been sent there—to bring some discipline and a sense of team work to her daughter's world.

After straightening out Hayley's room, Beth took one more look. While she cast her eyes around the room, there was something under her daughter's bed that caught her attention.

What's this? Beth bent down and pulled out a grey suitcase. She never noticed it before. Not belonging to her nor had she given it to Hayley, Beth was curious to see what was inside. The suitcase was locked, so she retrieved a pair of scissors from Hayley's drawer and broke in. What she saw startled her. Inside lay a collection of Hummel figurines along with an oil painting and a silver tea set.

Chapter Thirty-five

SARAH'S BODY SEIZED WITH a mixture of shock and surprise at Beth's words.

"I can't believe it!" she cried at the news of her beloved heirlooms. "I'm shocked to hear it."

"Your shocked? I was beyond shocked. I couldn't even comprehend it. The first thing I thought was that this stuff didn't belong to Hayley, obviously. But whose was it? Then I remembered the robbery, and it all came together."

"But. . ." Sarah was at a loss for words. "Just why would Hayley do something like that? How did she get into my apartment in the first place?"

"I wondered the same thing. . .that is, until I found *this*."

Beth reached into her pocket and pulled out a dull pewter colored key. She handed it to Sarah.

Sarah examined it and said, "I think this is *my* key—the extra one, that is. I'm pretty sure the one I use is still on the key ring." She got up and went to the front door. Inserting the key, her jaw dropped. "It's my key, alright. . .wonder how it came into Hayley's possession?"

Beth shrugged. "Tell me."

"It's so weird."

"I know. So, I questioned Hayley about it."

"What did she say?"

"At first, she played dumb. But I basically interrogated her until she finally broke down and admitted what she'd done. She'd found it by your door. Said she'd heard once from Emily that there were some valuables inside. . .you know how kids talk and all." Beth paused. "I don't know how to apologize to you, Sarah, but—"

Sarah waved her hand. "Oh, please don't even. I know you feel bad, Beth, but they're just material goods. I had been pretty upset over thinking they were gone forever, but it was mainly the sentimental value is all—I mean, at least they're found now."

"I feel like crap having to admit all of this to you." Beth hung her head and wiped her eyes again with the shredded tissue.

"Here, take another one," Sarah insisted, handing a fresh box of tissues to Beth.

"Thanks," she said, pressing the tissue to her nose. "Also, she said something about accidentally knocking over a statue."

"Oh, yes, my great-grandmother's bust. . .I'd wondered how that got broken."

"I feel so terrible, Sarah."

Sarah came over to the sofa and put her arm around Beth. "Listen, I don't hold anything against you or Hayley. . .really, I don't."

Beth raised her head and a hint of a smile emerged. "Well, I'll just have to hold it against myself, I guess. You don't know how much I dreaded coming over to tell you all this. So embarrassing, really. But there's more."

Sarah couldn't imagine what else could be said. The robbery was solved. There was no more worry or fear about the break-in, and Sarah's heart lightened at the fact that she'd be able to get her things back again. The dollar value as well as the sentimental value were priceless. While Sarah had already put a down payment on the Greenbrier condo, now she'd be able to pay it back to the bank easily. She braced for more of what was on Beth's mind.

"Besides the suitcase full of your stuff, guess what else I found?" Beth's eyes popped in mock surprise. "Her journal—diary—whatever you want to call it these days."

Sarah's interest was piqued. "You broke into that, too?"

Beth nodded with exaggeration. "Oh, yeah."

Sarah's mind churned with the memory of her own mother opening up the diary that Sarah had kept locked in her drawer. The embarrassment of her mother reading her private thoughts stuck with her for a long time. The privacy invasion. . .the intrusion. . .it was all a bit much for a 14-year-old to be obligated to share her private feelings to anyone, especially her mother. The chagrin for being exposed for her innocent teenage angst was humiliating, and was even worse than the problems she'd secretly written about.

"What did you find?"

Beth took a deep breath. "Sarah, you know John Sterns, Winny's brother?"

Sarah nodded. "What about him?"

Beth's lips pressed in as she shook her head. The color now returned somewhat to her face, and she stood up with the resolve of a mother bear about to defend her cub. "That. . .that *bastard* has been using my little girl as his. . .oh, what do you call them?"

Sarah immediately thought drug runner or even worse, his *whore*. She didn't venture to answer the question, hoping Beth would quickly fill in the blank.

"I want to say his co-conspirator, but I'm pretty sure he was using her to get money for. . .for whatever it was he wanted."

"Drugs?"

"I don't know for sure, but, yeah, it was probably drugs. Whatever, he was using her, and that's the most egregious thing an adult could do to a young girl."

"Drugs. . .you know for sure?"

"It's all right there in the diary. . .right there on paper. . .her own words. Sounded like a perverted love story."

"He had sex with her?"

Beth stood and paced the floor in front of the coffee table. "I hate to think so, but it sounded like she was in love with the guy."

"John Sterns? He's old enough to be her father."

"Yep."

His demeanor had always left Sarah questioning, and his body language totally turned her off. He never gave her a second look after they talked in the hall the first day she met him. She wondered why he was always so dismissive of her after that. His gawky stare usually sent a chill through her—and not in a good way. She remained polite but reserved herself from engaging too much. Could his ego have been so deflated by such an innocent remark as, "I'm single but not looking right now, thank you." But to aim for someone like Hayley? That's jail bait material.

"Beth, you have a situation on your hands here."

"I know. Compounding everything else." She sat back down on the sofa and held her fingers to her temples.

"Are you going to press any charges. I mean she's underage and all."

With exasperation in her voice, Beth said, "I don't know. I really don't know at this point. With Hayley's issues and all, I'm spent. I've been pondering it day and night, but I don't know which way to turn first. I'm waiting on Tim's final word on it. He should be coming home from his business trip tomorrow."

Sarah took in all that she'd heard and tried to process it going forward. She couldn't imagine being in Beth's shoes right now.

"Oh, and when they picked up Hayley on the roadway, her knapsack contained two China figurines."

"Hmmm. . .wonder if they were mine?"

"They probably were, Sarah. They got a bit chipped though. I'm pretty sure she was going to try to sell them while away at the camp."

"I can't believe that guy. What a piece of work." Sarah seethed. "I'd always had my suspicions about him, but I could never quite put my finger on why. . .thought it was just my imagination."

"A woman's gut is rarely ever wrong," Beth surmised. "Believe me, I was suspicious of him, too. But his dear old sister kept me from saying anything. . .such a dear soul."

Sarah crossed her arms over her chest. "I hope he's treating her better inside those closed doors than outside. Because his outside demeanor sucks. He always seems so short tempered, or like he's in a hurry."

"Hurry to go nowhere. . .such a loser. Doesn't even have a job." Beth picked up her coffee cup from the table and took a sip. She proceeded to tell Sarah all that she'd read in her daughter's diary and the details of her relationship with John Sterns.

After talking for an hour or so, Beth stood. Sarah mirrored her and reached out to give the woman a hug.

"Hey, listen," Sarah began. "We're not just neighbors, we're friends and we have been for a while now. Your problems are mine, too. So, please feel free to let me know when you need my help. Looks like I'll be moving at the end of the summer, but our friendship will remain, you hear?"

With a sniffle, Beth nodded, tightening her arms around Sarah.

How sad to now have to deal with so much at one time. Sarah comforted Beth for a while in the living room and they prayed together. She didn't ask when she'd get her items back as it seemed so insignificant in light of all Beth was going through. Shortly, after Beth left, she returned holding the suitcase and handed it to Sarah at the door. At that point, the heirlooms felt more like a consolation prize rather than a joyous moment for Sarah. Nevertheless, the joy of seeing the old family treasures slowly came back to her.

Chapter Thirty-six

Present day. . .

SARAH PICKED UP A box with the words, *Emily's room,* written on it in black marker. "Okay, Em, I also need you to please put all of the boxes with your name written on them in your room as well as the others I mentioned," Sarah instructed just as her cell rang. "I'll manage the rest for now." Sarah set down the box and lifted the cell out of her pocket. Her heart lightened at seeing the caller ID. It was Nick. They'd chatted a couple of times since she left the hospital. She couldn't understand the pattering of her heart could be so palpable after seeing him come into her room that day. Had his role in finding Emily created a hero out of him? Was it the pain-relieving meds that softened her heart? Why the change to the point of her being stirred at just hearing his voice? Though by now, it didn't matter because her heart tugged in his direction, and there was no way to stop the momentum. It was as though she'd taken a whole new lease out on her life, and it was co-signed by Nick Durham.

"Hey," she cooed into the phone.

"Hey, yourself," Nick replied. "What's up for today?"

"Ugh, I'm up to my neck in boxes."

"Need some help there? I can come—"

"No, no, you've done enough with the furniture already."

"I'm more than just a furniture guy."

She smiled. "I know."

"What d'ya say, I come over and help? Afterward, maybe we can all go out to dinner?"

Sarah's heart melted. Just the thought of him wanting to help her was enough to make her day. Having dinner, too, with Emily included, made her feel like they were a family. Who knew how the intricacies of the heart worked, but God had really changed him. Or was she the one who changed?

****

At Giuliani's restaurant, Sarah and Nick, along with Emily, sat on the patio overlooking the expansive gardens. Dining *al fresco* always made the food taste a little better in Sarah's opinion. Tucked under a canopy of trees, a chorus of melodious birdsong high above underscored the stunning ambiance. Sarah took in the pristinely appointed garden as she admired the landscaping. Manicured lawns, topiaries, and the touch of a sparkling fountain lent the feeling of a European estate. The moment was ethereal; it all seemed like a bubble had surrounded them and nothing could pierce it. She mused at how wonderful the moment was and how far they came since her devastating accident and Emily's brief disappearance. This amazing moment was beyond her understanding.

"This place is gorgeous, Nick," Sarah gushed. "How'd you find it?"

Nick shrugged. His lips held a silent smirk as though he were hiding something from her.

"I know!" called out Emily, her eyes beaming with joy.

Sarah thought she saw Nick glance at Emily and even wink—maybe?

"What's that about?" Sarah asked.

"Nothing," Nick said. The corners of his mouth turned up.

Just then the waitress approached the table. The sweet aroma wafted by as she placed their orders in front of them. "Anything else?" she asked, politely.

"Looks like we're good," Nick said.

Sarah took a bite of her veggie burger while keeping an eye on Nick and Emily. They'd always gotten along well, but there was something in the air. Emily seemed to enjoy her California burger and Nick apparently wasn't hungry judging by the way he'd only pushed the food around his plate. Sarah wondered what was going on.

"Everything okay?" she asked him.

Nick looked up and gave her a quick nod. "Yep, all good here. . .why?"

"You seem fidgety."

He gave her an awkward grin while ramming his straw into his glass causing the ice cubes to clink.

"Right there." She pointed to his glass as the ice cubes tumbled around and around. He quickly stopped poking and stirring the cubes and took a chug. "Just wanted to get all the soda down into the glass."

"Okay, whatever. . .but you haven't eaten much on your plate."

He looked down at his food. "Sure, I did."

"You left half your burger. Is it too rare or. . .?"

He picked up the top of the bun to inspect. "Somewhat gristly is all."

"A little gristle?" She smiled. "Since when did that bother you?"

He raised his eyebrows and shrugged. "Yours okay?

Sarah pointed to her near empty plate. "I think this says it all."

He looked over at Emily. "Seems like you liked your burger, too, right Em?"

She nodded and shoved the soda straw between her lips.

Nick slapped his hands on his thighs. "Okay, so what's up for the rest of the day, ladies? Where do you all want to go—out for ice cream? Miniature golf?" He glanced at his watch. "It's still early."

Sarah eyed him and then Emily. "What do you say, Em?"

"I don't know, Mom. What do you guys want to do?" Emily looked back and forth between her mother and Nick.

"I know what," Nick began. "How about someone proposes?"

Just then the waitress brought a small tray over to the table and placed it in front of Sarah. When she saw the red rose and black box, she froze. The reality of the moment sent her heart into overdrive. Swept up with emotion, her eyes teared as she turned to Nick.

"W-what's going on?" she stammered.

Nick raised both hands as though resigned that he didn't know. "Looks like a flower and a box there." His lips spread into a tentative smile.

Sarah blushed and then opened the tiny black box. She gasped. Inside lay a solitary diamond ring.

"Sarah, "Nick began. He reached over and lifted out the ring. "Um, I've been afraid for a while to get too close to you. I mean. . .when we were together—you know, before." He waved his hand dismissively. "I guess, that was my problem all along. I was—well, just afraid is what I was. I didn't want to push you away so much as just guard my heart." He took her by the hand and held the ring with the other. His face blushed bright red as he got down on one knee. "But I've changed, Sarah. . .ever since I almost lost you, I realized that I don't think I'd be happy without you in my life." Nick paused. Sarah's heart nearly burst at what was coming next. "Would you do me the honor of marrying me?"

Sarah trembled. Holding back her emotions, she closed her eyes and nodded. It was all she could do at the moment. He slipped the ring onto her finger. Tears pooled in her eyes.

"Yes, Nick," she managed to say in a whisper. "I'll marry you."

Chapter Thirty-seven

"THESE ARE SO GORGEOUS," Sarah mused as she ruffled through the collection of wedding gowns. Row upon row of luxurious silk and satin dresses drenched in tufts of lace and tulle by the mile draped the racks at Salon Di Moda.

"I know," Cindy said. "Beautiful. . .but it's hard pick just one. Hey, look at this one." Cindy pulled a bateau-laced bodice with sequined see-through sleeves.

"Wow, love it."

"I know, awesome." Cindy continued searching through the racks. "Too bad I'm not getting married," she chuckled. "I mean—again."

"Where are the less formal ones?"

Cindy let go of the sleeve of the dress she'd been ogling. "Hmmm, not sure."

"Hi, I'm Lena. Something I can help you with?" an attractive redhead said as she approached.

"Hi, yes. I'm getting married soon."

"Congratulations!"

"Yes, thanks. Well, it's my second marriage, so I won't be wearing white."

The redhead nodded, understandingly. "Oh, not a problem. We have several racks of informals." She gestured with a bright neon blue nail pointing to the far side of the showroom.

Sarah turned to get a look. "Oh, great. Thanks." To Cindy: "Hey, I'm going to check out the other dresses."

Minutes later, Sarah came out of the dressing room wearing one of the informals.

"Looks really good on you," Cindy said of the silk blue sheath dress, giving Sarah the *okay* sign.

Sarah ran her hands down the sides of the smooth material and turned around in the mirror.

"You really think so?"

Cindy smiled. "It's perfect. Nick will love it."

"Okay, but there's a couple more to try on." Sarah reached around to unzip the dress.

"I'll take it when you're ready," Lena said, extending her hand. "I'll put it aside for you."

Sarah handed the luxurious drape of blue silk to the woman. "Okay, Cin, the next one is great, too. Wait 'til you see it. Be right back."

"Take your time." Cindy pulled out her phone. "I'm in no rush." While Cindy waited for Sarah to come back out, she scrolled through Facebook, and as the minutes ticked on, she eventually opened up an online word game. She became engrossed in the challenge and eventually realized she hadn't seen Sarah come back out. What was taking so long? "Hey, you need help with anything in there, hon?" Silence. "Sarah, the runway is awaiting. . .the photographers are getting antsy here. . .Sarah?"

Cindy glanced at the rows of dresses all around her. Besides the red head, there were only two other women inside the dress shop. Cindy headed back toward the dressing room. "Sarah?" All remained quiet as Cindy went from room to room. "Sarah!" Cindy gasped at what she saw behind the curtain. Half-dressed in a lavender sequined gown, Sarah lay sprawled on the floor. Cindy panicked and screamed for the attendant. "Help! Please, help!"

Chapter Thirty-eight

"You're gonna be alright." Cindy held Sarah's hand as the medical technician fastened her onto the gurney. "Don't worry, hon. I'll call Nick, and Emily will be fine. . .don't worry." Cindy's heart raced out of fear for what was happening. Sarah had been through so much turmoil lately. How was this even happening? Whether Sarah was even conscious and hearing Cindy's voice was unknown. Cindy didn't a have a good feeling. *How in the world did Sarah fall unconscious?* Sarah lent her support the best way she could. . .even as much as talking the med techs into allowing her to ride along in the ambulance with Sarah.

The siren blared as it took off out of the parking lot. Cindy held a finger to her ear with one hand and with the other, held onto Sarah's. *God, please get us all through this.*

"Nick? Hi, it's Cindy."

"Hey, what's up?"

"Yeah. . .um, just wanted to tell you that Sarah and I were shopping today, and something happened when—"

"Anything wrong?"

"She's being taken to the hospital."

"What hospital? Why?"

"Bryn Mawr."

"What happened?"

"We were at a bridal salon looking at dresses, and she was trying some on and modeling them for us—the saleslady and me—and then she went back into the dressing room and didn't come back out."

"So, what happened?"

"She was unconscious, Nick. Found her just lying there. It was awful So, I immediately called 911. "I'm with her now, and we're on the way to the hospital right now."

✳✳✳✳

The sight of the ventilator outside of room 327 sent a stab to Nick's heart. It was all too much as he stood at the threshold to Sarah's room.

"How could things get so bad so quickly?" he asked.

Cindy grimaced.

Nick stared at the ventilator. "This can't be happening,"

"I don't think she should've been released from the hospital so soon."

"But she'd gotten better and—"

"Yeah, but."

"What?"

"I never mentioned this before, Nick, but I overheard one of the nurses saying something about one of the doctors."

"The surgeon?"

"I think so. Oh, what was his name. . .I forget now. Dr. Bryon. . .Byron?"

"So. . .you're saying he was negligent?"

Cindy shook her head. "I can't say for sure, but. . ."

Nick frowned. "That's what they do these days. . .shuffle them in and out as quickly as possible."

"I know. And if they don't have insurance, then it's bye-bye."

"She has insurance, I thought?"

"Pretty sure," Cindy replied.

"If not, she will as soon as we're married."

Cindy smiled. "I'm so glad you two were able to work things out."

Nick pursed his lips. "I thought I'd lost her."

"She was pretty messed up about it, too. I don't think she ever got over you."

"That makes two of us."

Sarah's nurse puttered around the bed, checking the IV. "Got company, Miss Sarah," she said, glancing over her shoulder. "I'll see you soon, honey. Get some rest now."

As the nurse passed, Nick caught her attention. "Excuse me," he began. "I was wondering if. . ." He pointed to the ventilator in the hall. "Will my girl—um, Sarah—be needing that?"

"Oh, no, no. . .not to worry. That was for the other patient who was in here before."

The tension in his gut immediately released like a deflating balloon at hearing the nurse's words. "Glad to hear it," he replied with relief.

Cindy patted his arm. "You wanna go in now?"

He nodded.

"Things will all work out, Nick. You just need to have some faith here."

"I can only hope."

"Yep, goes for all of us."

Chapter Thirty-nine

SARAH'S EYES FLUTTERED OPEN at the sound of a pleasant voice.

"Hey, woman!" Cindy spoke in a raised whisper as she approached Sarah's bed. "Well, you're looking much better than the last we saw you. You've got some color in your cheeks now."

"Right," Sarah said and rolled her eyes. "I must've been a sight."

"Give yourself a break, Sarah."

"Hey, sweetie," Nick said, as he approached her bedside. Sarah's lips spread into a broad smile at the sight of him as he bent down to give her a kiss. "How's my girl?"

"Oh, Nick, I'm so sorry."

"About what?"

She lifted her arm and limply let it fall back down. "For this! I'm a mess, just a mess."

"Nonsense, just a little set-back is all." Nick glanced at Cindy. "We just need to have a little more faith, right?"

Cindy nodded. "I second that."

Sarah gave a meek smile before allowing her eyes to drift shut.

"Not to mention. . .you're getting married, woman." Cindy grinned.

Sarah's eye flew open. She turned her eyes toward Nick, who raised his eyebrows at her and nodded.

"Oh, Nick." Sarah whined, sweetly.

"What's this. You bailing on me?" His eyes twinkled.

"I need to be healthy. . ."

"Shhh, please don't cry, honey. We've been over this before."

"But. . ."

"Yes." Nick affirmed with a sweet smile. "Yes, you are. Rather, yes, *we* are."

"But I need to get well first."

Nick grinned, widely. "I'll take you any way I can."

Cindy nodded. "You will get well, Sarah. You'll see."

Sarah aimed her pointer finger toward the ceiling. "From your lips to God's ears."

Cindy gave a thumbs up sign. "Amen to that."

"Besides, we still need to get that beach house we always talked about, remember?" Nick raised his hands up as though resigned to it. "How're we going to afford it if we don't pool our money?" He winked.

Sarah recalled the beach house they imagined purchasing back in the throes of their new love. Pipe dreams were sweeter then when there were no other obstacles in the way. Florida had been the destination. . .the place she'd visited so often as a child with her parents. Her father's aunts owned twin bungalows attached by a long bright and airy breezeway. Sarah fondly recalled slipping down the hardwood floor right into the gallery where her Great Aunt Louisa's paintings and sculptures were kept.

Just then, Sarah's doctor stepped into the room. "Sarah. . .I'm Dr. Layton." He patted the bedrail. "Just wanted to give you a heads up on what's going on."

A hush came over the room. Nick and Cindy stood on the opposite side of the bed from the doctor, and all eyes riveted to him. "Since your splenectomy—let's see, that was about seven or eight weeks ago." He stared at the chart. "Alright, then. Well. . ." Dr. Layton quickly scanned the data while running his finger down the page. "I see that your previous doctor, a Dr. Byron, performed the operation. . .all seems okay here. Now, at this point, seems you have some signs of a low White Blood Count. . .it's 25.2. . .so, we'll need to put you on a strong antibiotic. I would have done that immediately after the surgery as your WBC numbers were low even before you were admitted here according to your data." His face etched in concern. He wrote something on her chart and then proceeded to check her pulse and ask more questions. ". . .Like I said, we would have kept you a bit longer."

"Bryn Mawr has a better reputation than most of the hospitals around, here," Cindy offered.

Dr. Layton lent a tight smile. "That's what we aim for."

"How long will I need to stay in bed, doctor?"

Dr. Layton pressed his lips together. "Well, I'd say as long as it takes—that is, as long as it takes for your WBC to go back to normal or near normal. I'm going to order some tests. . .a PCT and a few others. We'll take it one step at a time." He made another notation on the chart. "Also, as you don't have a spleen—as you know it's the organ that helps with blood filtration and infection control—all the more important to take every precaution to keep possible infection at bay, especially after a patient's operation where the immune system is not operating in perfect homeostasis—not quite up-to-speed. The PCT test should assess how things are going." He whipped off his glasses and met her eyes with his. "I suspect there may be an infection."

Sarah's face fell. "Infection?"

The doctor nodded. "I'm suspicious of some kind of abscess."

"Was it there before? Like. . .how long has it been there?"

The doctor took a deep breath and audibly exhaled. "Hard to tell. I could surmise here but I don't want to pass any judgment on prior medical protocols. Like I said, I'd have kept you under a different watch and care. But for now, you'll definitely need an antibiotic. That's a given, and I think we should hold off on having any surgery for now." He nodded. "We'll take a wait-and-see approach here. That's the most conservative route I can suggest. But because of your low blood count and your breathing issues, I'm going to put you on a C-PAP machine until the infection is resolved."

"I hope it clears up soon, doctor. I'm planning on getting married soon."

"Yes, she has a wedding in six weeks," Cindy chimed in.

The worried look on the doctor's face softened a bit. "Let's hope for the best," he said with a brief grin as he patted her arm. "I'm all for weddings."

Chapter Forty
One month later. . .

"Hey, what about this one?" Cindy held up a silky blue dress with glittery threads from the designer rack. "Too much or. . .?"

Emily cocked her head and a smile drew to her lips. "I kinda like it, Aunt Cindy."

Cindy beamed to herself. *Finally, a winner.* "Hey, Sarah. . .think we found one."

Sarah stood across the aisle in the shoe department. "Great. . .the lady's checking on a shoe for me. . .be right over."

Emily took the dress into the dressing room while Cindy hovered outside. "How's it look, sweetie?"

The door opened. The dress looked beautiful as Emily modeled it.

"I love it," Cindy said. "Looks perfect."

Emily's face appeared somewhat resigned.

"It looks great, Em, what's wrong?"

Emily shook her head. "I'm okay."

"No, really. You can tell me."

"I'll be fine," she insisted.

Cindy thought better than to press the issue, though she had a feeling Emily's mood had something do with her mother. Or perhaps Nick's involvement in their lives. Cindy wondered if Emily was happy or grieved that her mother would be marrying again. Was Emily pining for her father or comparing him with Nick? Or did she think her relationship with her mother would wane by virtue of the new man in their lives?

So many questions hovered in Cindy's head, rousing her curiosity, and she realized Emily wasn't herself from the moment they stepped into the mall. Even though Sarah was out of the hospital after having a rough time over the summer, Emily's worry about losing her mother just as she'd lost her father five years earlier could also be a plausible reason for the girl's concern. It was only natural for a fifteen-year-old to struggle with a fear of abandonment. Understandable for a vulnerable young girl with only one parent. Cindy wanted to put a band aid on Emily's heart, and in an effort to appease the situation without drawing out her fears any more than necessary, Cindy tread lightly.

"Is it about the wedding? You're happy for your mom, right?" Cindy stepped toward the entrance to the dressing area to keep an eye out for Sarah coming back.

"Yes, of course," she enthused. Nick's the greatest. . .even wants to adopt me."

"Oh, Em, that's wonderful news! How cool is that?"

"I know."

"He'll be a great dad, I'm sure."

"I'm not sure whether to call him Dad or keep calling him Nick." She smiled.

"I'm sure you'll figure it out, honey."

Anyone could see her fondness for Nick had slowly weened her from the fatherless gap she'd had since her own dad passed away as she bonded with Nick so easily. He'd been a godsend. He always managed to give her some attention and not ignore her on his visits to see Sarah. Being a cop, he'd given her the royal treatment and once let her ride in the squad car. His fondness for her was all too evident as he'd do anything for her mother, and anything that was dear to Sarah, he'd treat as tenderly if it were his own.

Now that her mother and Nick's wedding day drew near, Cindy hoped that any fears about Sarah's health that had earlier plagued Emily—not to mention all of those close to her—would soon dissolve at the pending joy of wedding bells and a happy future while everything else paled like twilight.

"Here comes your mom," Cindy said as she waved to Sarah. "Hey, we found a dress."

"Really, that's great."

Cindy pointed to the dressing room. "She's in there."

Sarah knocked on the dressing room door. "Hey, girly, let's see your dress."

Emily opened the door and Sarah's eyes widened.

"Wow, that's definitely you, Em. I love it." Sarah reached out to feel it. "So soft and it matches your eyes. Yep, it's a winner." Emily turned around and looked in the mirror again. Sarah hovered behind her, admiringly. "It's definitely you, honey. We'll take it."

Suddenly, Sarah put her hand to her forehead.

Cindy frowned. "You look a bit pale, Sarah. Are you alright. . .do you need some water or. . .?"

"Not sure, but I think I need something."

Chapter Forty-one

As SARAH LAY QUIETLY in yet another hospital bed, thoughts about the course of her life spun like a bad dream. *Why, Lord? What did I do to deserve this?* She hated the bed, the situation, and, most of all, herself. This was not the way she expected her life would roll, but life is not a fairytale, and she'd had her share of hard luck. *When will this all end?* She mused on the situation when Nick appeared in the doorway. As he entered the room, she quickly wiped any signs of tears away and hoped that she wasn't too hard to look at under the sharp fluorescent lights. Nick stepped up to the bed and bore a sweet smile. He picked up her hand.

"Feeling better now?"

Sarah shook her head. "This is getting old."

As Nick looked at her, the love in his eyes melted her heart.

"First, the accident. . .then the botched operation. . .and now this?" Her voice broke.

"Shhh. . .everything will work out the way it's supposed to," Nick reassured and squeezed her hand.

"Knock, knock," came a voice at the doorway. "Sorry to interrupt you lovebirds." Cindy grinned and entered the room.

"Hey, Cindy," Nick called.

"How's everyone doing here?"

"Hanging in," Nick replied.

After a long silence, Cindy said, "Hey, here's an idea I've been pondering. Why don't you guys get married here?"

"Here? In the hospital room?" Sarah waved her hand. "Oh, that's so ridiculous. How am I going to get married in a hospital room?"

"People do it all the time," Cindy explained.

"Who? Who does that?"

"I saw it once on a YouTube video."

"Every woman's dream, right? To get married in bed."

Cindy shrugged. "Just an idea. . .I guess a bad one."

"No, no. I know you're trying to help, Cin." Sarah reached out to pat Cindy's arm as she stood by the bed. "Whatever will be will be. If it's to happen here at Bryn Mawr Hospital, let it be. I mean, what choice do I have?"

"That's the spirit," Cindy said, giving her a thumbs up.

"Well, my dress won't be white that's for sure. . .there's already enough white in this room."

"The blue dress will be awesome—the one we picked out to match Emily's, and I know the hospital has a lady who comes in a couple of times a week and plays the piano—Rebecca Just Wagner—she'll agree to play." I'm sure they can bring a piano into the room or the hallway, so there'll be music, and Pastor Rogers can officiate. It'll be great." Cindy clasped her hands together. "And I'll be in charge of the flowers and decorations."

"Of course, you will. Who else?" Sarah smiled as she blinked back a tear. "I really don't know what I'd do without you—and Nick." She looked into his blue eyes and wondered if this was just some weird dream.

"Hey, that guy. . .does he look familiar to you?" Cindy pointed to the TV hanging from the wall.

Sarah looked up. "Oh, my gosh, that's him. John, my neighbor!"

Nick, Cindy, and Sarah all stared up at the newscast where the lead anchor talked about the arrest of John Sterns on charges of kidnapping and extortion, among other nefarious acts.

"Your neighbor?" Nick asked.

"From the apartment. You remember Winny and her brother, right? The lady with the palsy?"

"Oh, she was too sweet. I loved her," Cindy said.

"Me, too," Sarah added. "You remember her, Nick?"

"Vaguely."

"They lived, or *she* probably still lives down the hall across from Beth. I should call her, poor woman. Anyway, he's the guy that had that illicit relationship with Hayley Benson—our neighbor. . .Beth's daughter and Emily's friend." Sarah pursed her lips when a picture of John flashed on the screen. "Scum. . .that's what he is."

"So, Hayley was the other girl that went missing along with Emily," Cindy mused.

"Yep," Sarah answered.

"Wow, and *he* was responsible for her disappearance?" Cindy asked, keeping her eyes on the screen.

"Well, no one knows for sure, but I'm sure that he was involved somehow. If not him, someone who worked for him or was in cahoots with him. So sad about what happened to her."

Cindy gave a puzzled expression. "What exactly happened?"

"The night the girls went missing. . . apparently, they had been stalked by him or his look-alike. Emily told me she thought it may have been John but she wasn't one hundred percent sure."

"Oh, I remember that part, but what happened to Hayley?"

"The story goes that she and Emily went in different directions. Emily was so blessed." She glanced at Nick, who stood staring at the TV. "Nick was on the scene to help and everything," she gushed.

"Our hero for sure," Cindy patted him on the back.

Nick dismissed it by saying, "Ladies, I didn't save Emily, the two guys in the canoe were the ones. I just happened to be in the right place at the right time to greet her. Those guys deserve all of the credit."

"Sure, sure. . .so modest he is." Cindy grinned at him.

Nick held up his hand. "It's true, Cindy, and you know it."

"Okay, okay, whatever," she replied.

"But listen," Sarah continued. "Hayley apparently got caught by the guy at some point as she was running away. Emily headed toward the river, but Hayley went down the main street, so the story goes, and that's when he ended up grabbing her. That's what I heard from Beth, anyway."

"Oh, it's just so awful. . ." Cindy said.

Sarah took a mental leap back to the day when Emily was found safe. The emotional torture Sarah bore that night not knowing where her daughter was had sent her tumbling over a cliff of desperation. When it was all over, she thought to herself that it could have easily been the other way around. It could have been Emily in Hayley's shoes.

"So, this guy apparently stuffed Haley into the trunk of his car. No one knows why he did if all he wanted was the goods in her knapsack—you know, to sell the stuff she had on her for money."

"But how did John know that Hayley would be up at a hockey camp in Bethlehem of all places. I mean, that particular night?"

"They were dating—oh, that sounds so disgusting to say," Sarah winced at her own words. "Anyway, let me re-phrase that. . .they had *some* kind of relationship is all. He told her to bring some of the pricey goods with her. He was just using her as a glorified donkey."

"Aha. . .okay, now I get it." Cindy frowned.

"The police report stated what exactly? Nick, did you ever find out?"

Nick raised his eyebrows as he shook his head. "Looks like the guy stalked the wrong person. He was a rogue player apparently. Had no contact with John Sterns himself."

"So, he had no idea that Hayley was carrying anything of value in her knapsack?"

"Nope. Apparently, this guy was just some loner."

"Strange," Cindy said.

"So, how did John get caught. . .I mean, the drug ring and all?"

Nick nodded. "Hayley."

"Hayley?" Sarah questioned. "Really? They brought her in to testify?"

Nick gave a wry smile. "I guess she thought the kidnapping was his idea and she apparently didn't appreciate being stuffed in the trunk."

"Poor girl." Cindy muted the volume when the segment on John Sterns' arrest finished airing and the newscast went to a commercial break.

Sarah winced inwardly at the thought of her old friend, Winny, and the emotional pain she was no doubt going through now with her brother in jail. Sarah purposed in her heart to get in touch with the woman as soon as things got better health-wise.

"Seems everyone in John's sphere gets the raw end of things. By the way, you heard she's in a wheel chair, right?" Sarah said.

"Hayley?" Cindy asked.

Sarah nodded.

"Wow, really?" Cindy's eyes grew large. "That's rough."

"I know. And I think *I* have problems. Can't think of a worse problem right now than what the Bensons are going through."

Cindy put the remote down and turned to them. "So, guys, let's go to a safer space here. All this talk is bringing me down."

"So, what do you have in mind?" Sarah asked.

"Your wedding. . .hello?" Cindy palmed a mock wave. "Let's get back to what we were talking about, which was. . .oh, now I forgot."

"My wedding."

"No, no. I know that. Oh, wait. Yeah, the music. Like I said, I know this lady, Rebecca Just Wagner, who'd be happy to play. I can arrange the whole thing. Just let me know what music you want, and I'm sure she can accommodate anything you ask. Her sister used to sing with Liberace and everything."

"We can always wait until next year, Sarah." Nick squeezed her hand.

Sarah smiled. "If only. . ."

Nick's eyes met hers. "I know."

Chapter Forty-two

September 21

3:55 p.m.

THE MELODIOUS SOUNDS OF Mendelssohn resonated down the third-floor hallway of the C-wing of the hospital. The pianist sat in a small alcove across from Sarah's room where a piano had been placed. Her hands floated on the keys while the sleeves of her pink crepe blouse danced along with her movements. Several patients came out of their rooms and began gathering in the hallway to hear the music. Nurses and staff alike smiled as they wheeled patients up and down the hallway.

Cindy and Emily stood outside Sarah's room while Nick paced farther down the hall. The hospital administrative staff donated a huge flower bouquet and also a garland of roses, carnations, and baby's breath that draped around the doorway of room 342. Inside, Sarah sat up in her bed dressed in a beautiful tulle dress with pearls and sequins. One of the nurses sat on the bed with her applying make-up for the occasion. Sarah had wanted to stand up for the ceremony but everyone suggested otherwise. The risk of her getting dizzy or falling was too great. On his last visit, the doctor mentioned that she'd been hemodynamically unstable because of her anemia and low blood pressure, and there was still some kind of infection in her lower abdomen for which she wasn't a good candidate for surgery at this time. The antibiotics he'd prescribed needed to be stronger, so he'd put her on a higher dose after reviewing the lab result of the PCT test, which indicated a low White Blood Count of only 25.3 with a PCT of 3.4.

The expression, *don't put off to tomorrow what you can do today,* rang through Sarah's head the past few weeks. She'd vacillated for so long on what to do. . .wait or act now? One day, she just came to the decision that it was important enough to go through with the ceremony here and now. No one was guaranteed tomorrow. September twenty-first was the day she and Nick selected, and that was the day she would become Mrs. Nick Durham.

****

"You may kiss the bride," Pastor Jeffries said with a smile.

Nick leaned over the bed and planted a demure kiss on Sarah's lips. When he emerged, his face was pink and beaming. Cheers erupted from the folks who gathered by the bedside. Out in the hall, those who stood and watched from the doorway clapped, and a loud whistle rose above it all. Sarah was all smiles along with Nick as he raised her hand in his. Each of them bore glassy eyes that could barely hold back tears.

Chapter Forty-three

Five years later. . .
October 3
2:18 p.m.

NICK STARED OUT ONTO the ocean from the expansive window in the great room. The beach house had always been a dream for him and Sarah, and the angle from where he stood lent the best view. A salty breeze blew in the patio window as the ocean waves gently caressed the shoreline in the distance where the sun hovered over the water. In a few hours, when it would dip into the ocean, the blazing orange ball of light would sizzle on top of the waves. Sunset was Sarah's favorite time of day.

Nick took a step outside onto the patio. Amid the rush of the waves, all he could hear were Sarah's words about the wedding. . .her gushing about how perfect the day, the moment. . .that everything would be for an outdoor wedding at the shore. It had always been her wish for herself, but some things were not to be. Her voice rose above the splashing tide. "It's perfect. . .just perfect."

The scene took him back to the first time he and Sarah vacationed on one of the islands in the Caribbean—Antigua. Everything about that time together felt to him like ambrosia—the food, sun, air, and the love of his life in his arms. Life didn't get much better than being on an oasis in the middle of an expanse of water.

"Beautiful, just beautiful." Sarah's voice lingered in his ears along with the rush of the surf.

Indeed, it is. Nick fixed his eyes on the ocean.

The end of summer was the loveliest time to visit the shore, Sarah always reminded him. The crowds had dispersed by then from their vacations, and a quiet peace found its home again. Today, there wouldn't be as much peace and quiet as usual because Emily's wedding would take precedence in a few hours, and the beach home would soon thrum with the upbeat energy of friends and family.

****

Emily and Taylor, her maid of honor, busied themselves in Emily's room getting ready.

"Help me zip this, please," Taylor asked her mother. Cindy fussed with the zipper and finally got it to close.

"It's a little tight, honey," she said to her daughter. "Can you inhale for me? We should have let this out a bit."

Taylor inhaled. "It's fine, Mom. I haven't gained that much weight."

"I didn't say that you did. You look beautiful, honey. And you, Em. . . you look stunning," she said, admiringly. "Ethan is going to love it."

Emily blushed as she stood in front of a full-length mirror. She looked like an angel in her gown. The white satin and lace bodice draped across her shoulder in a bateau style. . .something her mother had also worn. The gown set off her shoulders nicely while keeping the collarbone from being exposed too much. The length of the train was just about three feet and remained tied up until the actual walk down the aisle.

****

Row upon row of white chairs sat lined up on white sheets layered across the sand. At the end of each aisle, jasmine and carnations draped along in spiraled garland. All of the guests dressed in beach clothes at the request of Emily and Ethan so they'd be comfortable.

Nothing like sand seeping into one's dress shoes or trying to balance in high heels.

The minister came out and asked every to stand. Emily's stomach whooshed with a flutter. All eyes would soon be on her and she felt a bit self-conscious. The white path leading to the alter was littered with white rose petals as the piped-in music started. She stepped onto the sand and was immediately greeted by Nick, who took her arm and escorted her down the aisle, which seemed longer than before when they'd rehearsed things. Nick had become so much like a father to her, and she was so proud to be on his arm. In his eyes, she saw that he held a faraway look that she'd never noticed before. *Was he happy or. . .?* He gave her a smile. Since it reached his eyes, she knew it was genuine. Yet there was something in it that she couldn't quite place—and then she did.

Up ahead Ethan stood next to his best man. He stood tall in his tux while his gaze fixed on Emily. She glanced over to Nick. If she wasn't mistaken, there were tears in Nick's eyes. As they proceeded down the aisle, at the end, Nick hugged Emily and said, "I'm proud of you," and then presented her to her groom. He placed Emily's hand in Ethan's and stepped away. Before he walked back to his seat, he patted Ethan on the shoulder. "Welcome to the family, son."

At the end of the ceremony, they kissed at the minister's invitation and walked down the aisle as all of the guests clapped. Everyone smiled and cheered. At the last aisle sat her Uncle Harry with a huge grin pasted on his flushed face. He waved as the couple walked by. Next to him sat the family's long-time friend and former neighbor, Beth Benson. Her husband, Tim, and daughter, Hayley, were there, too. Seeing the girl gave Emily's heart a tug as the memory of the fateful night alone in the woods flitted across her mind. Though at the same time, her emotions lifted at seeing Hayley standing alongside her parents and no longer bound in a wheelchair. Altogether, the moment was surreal. . .all of the smiling faces of her family and friends gathered at the ceremony. All for her and Ethan. Her joyous feelings overwhelmed her heart, especially her status as the new Mrs. Ethan Rogers.

Chapter Forty-four

October 4
8:07 a.m.

EMILY AND ETHAN STAYED overnight at the beach house until the next morning when their plane would leave for Antigua. Like her parents had talked about for themselves, Emily suggested to Ethan her desire to go to an island for their honeymoon. Ethan was all for it.

"Do you want to eat on the patio?" she asked him.

"Fine with me." He headed toward the bathroom. "I'll be out in a few minutes."

"Okay, breakfast should be ready by the time you're finished."

Emily went down the winding staircase leading to the first floor and turned for the breakfast nook that led into the kitchen.

"Morning, Dad," Emily called to him in the Great room as she passed through to the kitchen. From where she stood, she heard him talking. Emily put the water on for tea and oatmeal. She gathered the place settings on a large tray and washed some strawberries they'd purchased at the local farm market. While the oatmeal simmered, she put two pieces of toast in the toaster oven and poured orange juice into glasses for Ethan and herself. Emily then sipped her juice outside on the patio while enjoying the balmy morning breeze coming off the ocean. Later, she prepared the breakfast tray for them and brought it back out to the patio. Coming back inside once more, she heard her dad still talking.

"Yes, it was beautiful, darling," he spoke quietly while he stood in front of the fireplace. "She looked like a miniature you in her wedding dress—same hair, same eyes. . .I thought for a moment it was you." He smiled.

Just then, Ethan came down the stairs. "I'm starving. . .what's for breakfast?"

"Oatmeal, berries, toast and juice." She pointed to the patio. "It's outside. Help yourself."

"Sounds good, but aren't you joining me? Our first breakfast together and—"

"Yes, but shhh. . ."

"Why?" he whispered. "Why so quiet? What's going on?"

"Just go eat your breakfast. I promise to join you in a minute, okay?" Emily planted a kiss on his cheek and nudged him toward the patio. He gave her a funny look. "Just go, please. Your oatmeal is probably getting cold."

"Okay, okay, but I'll need an explanation later."

"You got it," she replied.

When Ethan left, Emily went into the Great room and stood at the threshold.

"I know I couldn't give you the wedding that you'd always wanted, Sarah," came Nick's voice. "But I want you to know that everything was perfect. . .as perfect as you'd always dreamed. In fact, it was better than I'd even imagined." He paused and smiled again. "Because you were there."

Emily stood listening to Nick. No one else was in the room.

"Dad. . .are you okay?"

Nick turned around. He looked surprised. His eyes enlarged, and he gave her a somewhat sulky smile as he stepped toward her. "Yes, honey, I'm fine. How are you?"

"I heard you talking in here, and I. . ."

"I was just talking. . .to your mother."

Emily came over to him and put her arm around his waist. Together, they looked up above the fireplace mantle to a picture of Sarah, Nick, and Emily. The picture was taken at the restaurant where Nick had proposed to Sarah years before. In the background, the garden's trees and blooming wisteria—Sarah's favorite flower—draped along trellises that rested by an old, stone edifice. Sarah liked it so much that she requested the photo be professionally enlarged and framed.

"You really miss her, don't you?" Emily studied him.

His eyes bore that same wistful look when he took her arm in his at the wedding. It couldn't have been clearer what had been on his mind—both then and now.

"You need to ask me that?" he said, and gave her a gentle one-armed hug.

"Not really, but I just didn't know what else to say."

Nick and Emily stood together in silence for a moment.

He turned to her. "You miss her, too?"

"You need to ask me that?" she said with a half-smile. Together, they turned toward the picture. A mild breeze floated through the screen door of the patio and made its way through the house. The scent of warm, salty air blended with jasmine filtered into the room. The scent was intoxicating to her. "It's perfect," Emily said to him.

Feeling the warmth of his body against her arm wrapped around him gave her pause to think how much she'd grown to love him. How blessed she and her mother had been to have him in their lives all these years. Those two short years they'd been married before she passed away had slipped by like a dream. Life is strange. If it hadn't been for her mother's tragic accident, Nick may have never come back into their lives. Of course, if she hadn't left the hockey camp that night, her mother may still be alive today. Emily pondered the weight of her actions in light of her present circumstances. While she couldn't take back that dreadful night, she did realize that while God took away her mother, he also blessed her with a second father and a husband, too. She'd heard her mother once say, *The Lord gives and the Lord takes away. We'll never understand God's plans or protocols because we're not God.* Tears drew to her eyes.

Nick turned to face Emily and placed his hands gently on her shoulders. His gaze met hers. "Yes, Em, it is perfect. Everything may not be exactly as I'd like it to be, but what I *do* have is perfect. Just perfect."

The End

www.ingramcontent.com/pod-product-compliance
Lightning Source LLC
Chambersburg PA
CBHW051129260626
47170CB00005B/1733

* 9 7 9 8 3 8 5 2 1 0 3 7 4 *